# THE

# DARROW BROOK

# FAIRIES

## BOB RICHEY

TWISTED TRUTH PRESS

Published by:

Book Cover by 'ZsaZsa'

Illustrations by 'ZsaZsa' ZsaZsa@Zsa--Zsa.com

ISBN: 978-1-970990-07-2   Paperback

Second edition 2025

## Dedication

This book is dedicated to all the people I mention in this book. Whether I called you by name, or inferred your participation, thank you for helping this memoir come to life.

I also wish to applaud the Darrow Brook Fairies for their excellent decision to allow this publication. The result may bring shockwaves to the paranormal community, but the possibilities of a future coexistence, outweigh the concerns.

iv

# THE DARROW BROOK FAIRIES

The Darrow Brook Fairies, is the true story of how I met the Darbries.

The story may be hard for you to believe, and the ways of these fairies may be very strange, but this is how I remember this happening from my youth.

I admit that I have been known to embellish my stories. I may have even told some downright lies to make my stories more fun, but this is my fair recollection of how these strange occurrences happened.

Of course I've recreated the dialogue, but only for the reason to convey the experience to you.

Enjoy!

# Preface

I wrote this story in Ellensburg, Washington. I am far, far away from Darrow Brook. I'm an old man now, and I write this fifty-year-old story from a faded memory. However, some of the story is as crystal clear as if it happened just yesterday.

Whether you believe it or not, it doesn't really matter. Enjoy the story. Always use critical thinking when you hear these tales about the unknown. Check the facts that you can! Investigate the parameters.

Many of the stories out there, especially about fairies, seem more made up than true. Ask yourself, how and why do they know this information about these creatures?

As for this story, I know little to nothing

about fairies. I've looked up Seely Curt fairies, with little luck finding truth. Big or small, mean or benevolent, I just don't know. What I can say is...

I know almost everything about the Darrow Brook Fairies.

# THE DARROW BROOK
# FAIRIES

## Index

# THE
# DARROW BROOK
# FAIRIES

## BOB RICHEY

I found myself sitting on the ground, leaning against an old hemlock tree. I was deep in the woods, facing the swamp. Tears were in my eyes, and I was holding my dead dog's collar in my hand, When I heard a strange flutter sound behind me.

Suddenly something flew past me and darted into the swamp. It moved in a blur, faster than you can imagine, but as it flew directly away from me, I thought I saw something.

It was just a Flash, but through the tears, I thought I saw a girl's bare bottom.

# Chapter 1

## The Property

In the mid-eighties, I bought a piece of land in northeast Pennsylvania. The bare land was on the border of Pennsylvania and New York State. I had made an offer to the owner, and he had refused it, going so far as to call me on the phone one night. In a drunken rant, he called me names and told me what he thought of my puny little offer. He called me again about a month later, and accepted the deal.

It wasn't prime real estate by any means. It was on a major state highway,

Route 430, but was deep in the countryside and very sparsely populated. There was only one other family and one old vacation home in the entire one-mile square.

About a quarter of my land was high and dry up by the road, and that made it easy to install a driveway. About half of the property was bare and sloped downward to the south. This land was fertile for crops but susceptible to being too wet in the rainy season or in overly wet years, making it unprofitable for regular farming. It was perfect for my ideas.

The back quarter was my favorite. At the end of the field, the woods began. A huge rock, affectionately named 'Thinking Rock,' was positioned on the path directly under the canopy of a huge old hickory tree. My daughter Kristin particularly loved this spot. There were three old hickory trees on the property. Two were on the edge of the woods and one further back on the other side of the creek. A charming creek flowed through the many large hemlock trees in the woods. The water in this creek flowed directly into French Creek, not far from where Darrow Brook branched off.

The woods were bordered by an old pasture to the south that extended one mile straight back to the other side of the square. To the east was a big forest in New York State, some of which was a stand of pine trees all planted in rows. It was planted in the forties as part of the New Deal's Civilian Conservation Corps tree-planting initiative.

The position of the forest so close to my property made it easy to hunt in Pennsylvania and then take a short walk to hunt game in New York State.

To the west, the square was divided by French Creek and, more importantly, Darrow Brook. Deep in the center of the square, Darrow Brook became more of a swamp than a creek. In fact, it was a huge swamp that was consistently impassable. The swamp was thick with vegetation, and walking through quickly became impossible. The mud was too deep, sucking your boots or shoes right off, and any of the drier, higher ground was filled with swamp bushes. A small path and openings, far too small for a person, probably made by rabbits or muskrats, were the only way to traverse the vast swamp.

I loved the woods bordering my ten-acre piece of property and enjoyed my life there as I ran a landscape construction company. I happily explored and hunted the forest I called home.

# The Darrow Brook Fairies

# Chapter 2

## Daisy

Daisy was an Old English Sheepdog. My mom owned a kennel down the road, and Daisy was her dog. She had another sheepdog as a pet in her apartment, and a cocker spaniel, so when Daisy continually wanted to go home with me, one day my mom said, "Go ahead, take her with you if she wants to go." Daisy jumped into my truck and sat in the passenger seat, enjoying the ride.

Daisy never looked back; she enjoyed the new place and the freedom to be outside. She watched the three boys anytime they played outside. She went with me many times back to the kennels to visit my mom, but she never missed a beat in jumping back into the truck and heading home.

Daisy was somewhat old when I got her. The only reason my mom allowed me to take her was that she had become too old to breed and have puppies. She wasn't bouncy or rambunctious as a younger dog might be; instead, she would lie quietly under the table or in a corner, barking at the slightest noise but calming back down quickly.

I lived alone when I first got her; she became my best friend. I didn't realize how badly I needed her to be around until I got her. She kept all loneliness away.

When my girlfriend and her four kids moved in, Daisy fit right in. She continually watched the children when they played outside. Daisy could always be found at a vantage point, giving her a view of them all. If Daisy was close by, so were all the kids. If Daisy was farther away, we knew the kids were spread out, so we'd call them to stay closer to the house.

On one such occasion, Daisy was barking incessantly. That was not like her, and my girlfriend and I quickly went outside to investigate what was wrong. Daisy was barking at the back, on the start of the path to the woods. You couldn't see much as the corn in the field was quite high, but we raced down the path past Daisy. Daisy held her ground, watching the other children as my girlfriend found the toddler and scooped him up.

There were other instances of Daisy herding the kids, but none as profound as the protection at night.

Daisy would always sleep in the hallway at night. The baby went to bed first, and Daisy would sleep in his doorway, blocking the path. You could not go back in there without nudging Daisy. She had to be nudged to move, but she would always go right back and take her position. When it was bedtime for the two older boys, she would move into the hall before their door, guarding both their door and the baby's. The same held true when the oldest daughter went to bed; Daisy moved, now guarding all three rooms. Finally, our room was at the very end of the hall, and when we were all asleep, Daisy would sleep blocking the entire hall.

No one had noticed this behavior until my girlfriend pointed it out. "Watch where she moves and sleeps every night," she explained.

It was the same every night. It was fun to watch, and one night, as she was getting the baby ready for bed, I yawned and stretched and said goodnight as the whole family watched me fake going to bed. I walked all the way down the hall, took off my clothes, and got in bed under the covers. It didn't take long at all for Daisy to start barking. She barked and barked as if refusing this change in the schedule. She would not permit my going to bed out of order! I got back up, calmed and petted her, and returned to my favorite chair in the living room before she calmed down.

I'd like to tell you more stories about Daisy, but this book was not about her. I just need you to know how endeared to her I was, and how sad I was when I found her up by the road, dead.

My heart sank to a depth it had never been. I openly bawled and lay down on the ground, hugging her. I lay there and cried for quite a while, listening beyond hope for a faint heartbeat, but there was none. Her eyes were open, and I touched one without a reaction. Crying, I carried her down the path and found a suitable place for her burial.

I went back to the house and got a shovel. No one was home but me. I thought about waiting for everyone to get home but decided against it. I called my mom and told her, then went down the path to bury my dog.

I dug a deep hole; the ground was easy to dig, but it took me longer as I continued to sob and cry. When I was finished, I removed her collar and spotted the charm I had bought on the first day when I got her from mom. It was engraved with Daisy and had the phone number on it. On the backside, it was adorned with rhinestones. It became my cherished keepsake to always remember her. I still cherish that tag.

I finished burying her and headed deep into the forest. I changed from sad to bawling and back again many times as I walked. I needed to be alone.

# The Darrow Brook Fairies

# Chapter 3

## The Swamp

I walked deep into the woods that afternoon. I found a favorite hunting area right next to the swamp. The ground was high, and there were many large hemlocks. The ground was bare except for the many old pine needles and pine cones. There were a few small bushes and plants scattered on the forest floor, but few, as the pine branches and canopies filled the sky and took up most of the sunshine. You could see quite far in all directions except toward the swamp. The swamp was like a wall of vegetation and water.

I found myself sitting on the ground with my back against one of those old hemlock trees, facing the swamp. Tears in my eyes and holding Daisy's collar in my hand, I heard a strange flutter sound behind me.

Suddenly, something flew past me and darted into the swamp. It was like a huge hummingbird, bigger than a raven but definitely not black. It seemed almost flesh-colored. It moved in a blur, faster than you can imagine, but as it flew directly away from me, I thought I saw something.

It was just a flash, but through the tears, I thought I saw a girl's bare bottom. I kept thinking, what the heck did I just see? I wiped the tears from my eyes, done crying, and decided it was a strange-colored bird and the tears in my eyes had blurred my vision. I decided it wasn't a girl but that I needed to investigate.

Facing the path where I last saw the bird fly, I dropped down into the swamp. The first few steps weren't that bad, even though I was sinking further and further into the mud. By the fifth step or so, my foot went so far down that when I pulled it back out, my shoe was still stuck in the mud. My shoes were brand new, so I maneuvered, found a way to reach down, and pulled it out of the mud. Slowly, I made my way back toward the bank, trying to be sure I didn't lose my other shoe.

I sat on the edge of the bank next to the swamp, scraping the mud off my legs and shoe. My right shoe was filled with water and mud, and I was trying to clean it enough to put it back on when I heard the splashing.

The splashing was loud. It sounded to me as if a herd of deer were running and splashing their way right toward me. It was getting louder and louder, but I could not see anything through the swamp bushes. When I finally saw it, I was surprised. It was about a foot long and swimming on the top of the swamp water, splashing with all four legs and its tail as it approached me. I backed up and was now standing on the top of the bank as it continued to approach. I was astounded as it started coming out of the water. It was a fish! It was about a foot long, with slimy, mottled skin and four stubby legs, swimming and splashing on the swamp water's surface, and it was ugly. It was horrifyingly ugly, and it was still coming up the bank toward me when I started to run. One shoe on and one shoe off, I ran for home.

I hadn't run far when I stopped to put on my wet shoe. Sitting on the ground, I squeezed my foot into the sloppy shoe and, as I got up, I picked Daisy's collar back up. It was then that I noticed her tag was missing.

My heart sank. That was the last thing I wanted to lose. I started walking back to look for it but quickly remembered the ugly thing chasing me and the fact that it was starting to get dark, and I didn't have a flashlight or anything.

I stumbled back home and ended the day by telling everyone Daisy had passed and showed them where she was buried. Everyone was openly sad for a week or so. We sure missed Daisy.

# Chapter 4

## Daisy's Tag

The next day was a Sunday, and I explained to my girlfriend what I had to do as I packed a sandwich and some beers in my hunting vest. I took off for the swamp in late morning to retrace my steps. I had high hopes of finding Daisy's nametag.

It was a long way back to the place I realized I'd lost it, and I had mentally marked the spot in my mind. I looked into the swamp and all around, hoping to catch sight of a deer or a fox. At least, that's what

I kept telling myself. I was secretly hoping to spot the creature I thought I saw flying, though I told myself I was only looking for Daisy's tag.

Mentally marking the spot didn't work at all. I couldn't find it. It hadn't occurred to me that I would need to stop in the exact same place, in the exact same direction, with the exact same lighting to be sure of the spot. I couldn't find it at all. I made a mental note that, on the way back, I would keep searching the ground from here to the house if I didn't find the tag. I piled some rocks and proceeded to walk toward the stand of hemlocks, searching the ground for something shiny the whole way.

I got to the general area where I had seen the bird-girl fly into the swamp; I realized that I could not be sure of the exact tree I was sitting against. I hadn't marked it, and the big hemlock trees all looked alike. The swamp looked the same too. I couldn't find the spot, even after searching. I walked up and down the bank of the swamp over and over, unsure if I was too far or not far enough in.

The ground was dry but damp under the fresh layer of pine needles blanketing the ground. Rain the previous night had dislodged a fresh layer of pine needles, and more needles and pine cones were still falling from the trees as the wind blew and swirled.

I soon realized that, although I covered a lot of ground, I had to mark an area and search for Daisy's tag in a methodical manner.

I piled up some rocks and started to search but quickly realized that it could already have been covered up with pine needles. It would be hard to find her tag for several reasons. The forest floor was covered in shade. Very few patches of sunshine made it to the forest floor. The glint of the shiny tag would be easier to find in sunlight. My stomach sank when I thought that maybe a crow had found it and picked it up. I could not see any crows, but I had heard them cawing all morning. There were many crows.

I kept looking as I thought about the squirrels and the many chipmunks I had seen and heard that day. I tried my best to ignore all the remote possibilities and concentrate on finding the tag.

I looked into the swamp often, searching for the spot where I had seen the bird-girl disappear. It all looked the same now. There wasn't any tree or landmark that would make the spot stand out or help me be sure I was in the right spot, so I just continued to search.

The search turned both futile and frustrating. I couldn't find the tag anywhere. It had vanished into the forest floor. I decided that I needed a metal detector and would bring one out with me next time I searched. I sat down again, leaning against a tree, and ate half of my sandwich and drank a beer. I was frustrated, but the gentle breeze and soft chatter of birds and animals soothed my frustration, making anger nearly impossible. Tag or not, this was truly a great place to relax and think. That's what I was doing when the woods went quiet.

It happened all of a sudden. There was no warning. Everything was normal, with chipmunks and squirrels scurrying around, making noise as they rustled the grass and pine needles on the ground. They chirped out signals and sounds constantly. The birds fluttered and chirped too. They flitted and flew through the limbs and branches, landing and resting, then taking flight again. The ongoing sight and sound of the entire woods instantly became silent. Nothing moved. Nothing made a sound. Even the breeze through the trees seemed to stop.

I froze too. What was happening, I thought. I looked all around until I finally saw it. A shadow was flickering along the forest floor, coming straight toward me. I looked up and saw it. It was huge! With a wingspan of around ten feet, the owl glided silently through the trees.

The owl suddenly flapped its wings and landed on a branch a few trees away from the one I was sitting against. It sat there silently, turning its head back and forth, looking for a meal.

Not today, I decided. I jumped up and started shouting, "Go away!" I waved my arms and approached the tree it was sitting in, but it merely looked at me. I picked up sticks and threw them at the owl, missing wildly but getting closer and closer, and soon the owl had had enough, and I dislodged it from its mighty perch.

"Go! Get out of here!" I yelled. "You're scaring all the other animals."

I watched as it flew deeper into the woods. Soon, all I could see was the flicker of sunlight on the forest floor, and then it was gone.

I sat back down at my tree and opened another beer. "Phisssst!" That sound in the silent woods could have been heard a mile away. I took a sip and yelled to the wind, "I did that! That's all on me! You can all come back out! I scared it away!"

I chuckled as I realized my yelling was only making it worse, and I sat quietly, waiting for the forest to return to normal. As I waited, drinking my beer, I thought I heard the wind in the branches say, "Jude man."

Maybe it said, "Good man"? It wasn't words; it was more like sounds, but it was strange and clearer than I'd ever heard the wind. Maybe it was because it was so quiet, or maybe because I was listening intently to hear the return of the chipmunk noises, but either way, the sound would haunt me. That's the nature of the swamp, I thought. Strange things happen out here. It was probably worse deeper in the swamp, I figured. I wouldn't want to spend the night there, or even right here, I decided.

It took a while, but the noises started to come back, and the animals returned to normal. Soon, the birds and squirrels were back at it, flitting and scurrying around. I finished my beer and got up, dropping the can on the ground with the first one. I stomped on both cans, squishing them down to fit in my pocket. I took the other half of my sandwich, picked it apart, and spread the crumbs for my new friends. I put the plastic bag into my pocket and headed off for home, scouring the ground for Daisy's tag the entire way. It was just getting dusk when I made it back home.

# Chapter 5

## First Contact

It took a couple of days before I could break free of work and go search for Daisy's tag again. I grabbed a beer and found the metal detector stashed in the work truck with the tools. We used it to find septic tank lids. Almost all septic tanks have metal handles embedded in the cement lids. The metal detector makes them easy to find, as the homeowner usually points out the location by memory. Some beer, a metal detector, and this time a flashlight were on my list. I wouldn't need it, I hoped, but it's always better to be prepared.

I enjoyed the walk out to the swamp. It was way more fun to go out there than to come back home. There wasn't a path to follow, certainly not a trail; I just walked through the woods in the general direction of where I wanted to go and was sometimes surprised that I had overshot or undershot where I thought I was when I finally reached the swamp. That wasn't unnerving like it was when returning home at dusk. Sometimes, upon reaching the opening where I expected to see my house, nothing looked familiar. It was starting to get dark, and I didn't know where I was. That was a scary feeling, but it only lasted a few seconds as I got my bearings and angled through the field until I saw my neighbor's house, then mine.

This walk was different, as I kept turning on the metal detector and testing it as I walked. It would beep, and I brushed back the surface leaves and needles to examine the ground. It beeped again, indicating something deeper under the dirt, and I hadn't brought a shovel or anything to dig with. I finally gave up and went directly to the swamp. I hadn't gone far enough, but because of all the delays looking for stuff, I thought I had walked too far. I walked back, trying to find the swamp area, and instead broke out into the field and could see my house in the distance.

I almost gave up for the day right there but, remembering the flashlight, decided to go back out, even though my schedule would barely get me home by dark.

I walked quicker than normal this time but I still kept looking around for the bird-girl.

Finally, I got back to the hemlocks bordering the swamp. I fixed my pile of marker rocks and started searching for the tag with my metal detector. The beeping didn't happen often, but when it did, it usually pointed to something deep underground. That wouldn't be the tag, I thought. I wished I could come out here sometime and find out what these metal pieces were buried along the swamp. But I knew the tag would be close to the surface, so I ignored the other hits and focused on signals that moved when I scooped off the surface debris, causing the signal to shift. Every time that happened, I got excited. Found it, I'd think at first, but after a few buttons and square-headed nails, I was beginning to think I wouldn't find it at all.

On one particular hit, the detector whined and beeped a couple times, then made a sound like a young girl's voice, "Find it." I looked in the needles but found nothing. "Find it!" I said, "I'm trying to find it!" I tested it again, and it made that weird whine back and forth, then, "Find it," again. I looked and picked out a nail. I tested the empty pile, and nothing. What was going on with this detector? I should mention, I bought this metal detector from a classified ad; it was supposed to be brand new but cost less than half price. When I bought it, it came in a brown cardboard box and was indeed brand new, but it didn't have a brand name anywhere on it. There was no writing on the box, and it came without instructions. So, when it said "Find it," I had no idea if it was a setting or not. I would have expected it to say "Found it" if the tone matched its settings for what I was looking for, but I had it set for any metal.

I sat down against a tree, fiddled with the settings, turned it off to save batteries, and opened my beer.

I was just sitting there, enjoying my beer, when I heard it again, "Find it." I froze. I could see the metal detector in front of me, and the light was off. The sound came from behind me, faint but unmistakable in the quiet woods. I thought about "Jude man," but this wasn't the wind. I sat there, silent and motionless.

"Darbrie, find it," it said, closer now. I thought to myself, there's a freakin' parrot in the woods.

"Darbrie, find it," it said again.

Wait a minute, I thought, was Darbrie the thing that crawled out of the swamp? "Did that monster steal my tag?" I spoke.

"No, silly, Darbrie find it," whatever was talking to me was right behind my tree. I readied to pounce but quickly changed my mind. I'll scare it, I thought, and I really, really want to see what it is.

I sat there and calmly said, "Do you know where my dog's tag is?"

"Yes," was all she said.

Suddenly, the flutter sound got louder, and the blur of the bird-girl flew quickly into the swamp again. I saw her tiny bottom much clearer this time, even though it was still just a blur.

I sat there, heart racing, wondering if that had really happened or if it was just a dream, when the woods went silent again. I looked around but didn't see anything.

Aaaaiiieeee: the sound of a hawk pierced the air. I stood up and watched. It swooped down, landed, and started sticking its head in a hole, trying to catch something under an old dead tree. I ran toward it, yelling and tossing sticks. I threw my beer can at it, and it thumped, bouncing off the log. The hawk looked up, saw me closing in, and flew off.

"Not on my watch!" I said aloud. "These are my friends around here."

I looked around and realized it was almost dusk. It would be dark by the time I got home. I knew I'd better get going.

I crushed the beer can, put it in my pocket, and dug out the flashlight. I tested it to be sure it was working and quickly made my way home. It got really dark in the woods, and I really needed the flashlight. I finally reached the clearing and could see the lights at my house.

Relieved, I got home to a huge bowl of chili. Almost all the ingredients were from the garden, and the meat was venison from last deer season. I ate hungrily.

"Well? Did you find the tag?" my girlfriend asked.

"Yes, well, kind of," I told her.

"What's that supposed to mean?" she asked.

"Well, I don't know how to explain it, and I doubt you'll understand or even believe me," I answered.

"I don't care what you do out there in those woods, you know that, don't you?" she said as she left the kitchen.

"I do now! And for the record, I don't know or care what you put in this chili, but it sure is delicious!"

I could hear her laugh and say, "Thank you," all the way down the hall.

# The Darrow Brook Fairies

# Chapter 6

## It's All a Dream

I couldn't wait for morning to come and get back out there. I tossed and turned all night. I had almost seen the bird-girl and kept picturing what she would look like. I pictured a winged creature with a feathered chest area and a bird's head with a long beak. It also had a cute, flesh-colored bottom that looked almost human. It would have legs like talons, and in one talon, it clutched Daisy's tag.

I got up early, canceled all my jobs for the day, and packed some food and beer. I grabbed the flashlight and glanced at my forty-four-caliber black-powder revolver hanging on the wall. I quickly decided against taking it. I did not feel the slightest bit threatened. I wasn't scared at all, even though the swamp could be very frightening. Plus, I didn't want to frighten the thing that seemed able to mimic a parrot, if not actually talk.

During the entire walk to the swamp, I closely examined every bird, searching for any hint of the bird-girl. Nothing seemed to come close. Had I discovered a new species? One that no one had ever seen? Maybe I'd be famous, but maybe I wouldn't be able to prove it. I didn't have a camera or any recording device. How would a recorder help? Surely, no one would believe a recording. I wouldn't. I considered the predators. It was obviously not a hawk, since a hawk had scared it off. It couldn't be an owl or a fox, especially not a fox, since a fox can't fly.

It could be like a hummingbird or a giant bumblebee, perhaps a cross between them. My mind was racing with ideas, and I only calmed down when I reached the swamp. I found my pile of rocks and sat down by a huge hemlock tree.

I sat there for hours. I drank a beer just to pass the time.

Soon, I convinced myself I was imagining things, perhaps having fallen asleep and dreamed it all, turning the strange noises and wind sounds through the trees into words. How foolish I was to let myself think there was a talking bird out here.

Dejected, I remembered that in grade school, Connie had claimed she had a talking crow. No one believed her, but she went on and on as if it were true. Maybe it was true. Maybe more birds than just parrots and parakeets can talk. Cockatiels can learn to talk, but those are a lot like parrots. Can magpies talk?

My mind was racing again, debating whether it was real or imagined, constantly shifting back and forth. Over and over, I changed my mind, when I heard it.

"Find Jude Man."

I could barely hear it in the wind, but I was sure I heard, "Find Jude Man."

Was I supposed to look for someone? What was a Jude Man? I sat motionless and perfectly quiet, listening to the wind. Suddenly, I heard it again, louder and closer.

"Darbrie, Find Jude Man!"

I sat up straight and looked around. "Where are you?" I asked.

There was no answer. I waited, then I asked, "Do you have Daisy's tag?"

"Yes," the answer came quickly.

"Where are you?" I asked again.

44

The fluttering sound was faint but louder than before. Darbrie, or whatever its name was, was close by, maybe right on the other side of this big tree.

"Can I have the shiny tag back?" I pleaded. "It's very important to me; it has great sentimental value." I immediately assumed that a bird would not understand that at all, no matter how smart it was.

"Yes, Jude Man," it answered.

I was hoping beyond hope that nothing would come around and scare it away again as I coaxed it out into the open.

"Can I have it back?" I said again.

"Yes, silly," it said. I heard fluttering, and then it said, "Hello."

I looked around but didn't see anything. "I can't see you," I said.

"Hello, Silly Jude Man." The sound came from above me.

I bent my neck to look straight up and saw her. Well, all I saw was her face. It was the prettiest face I had ever seen, perfect in all ways. She was the most beautiful girl I had ever seen. I felt dizzy, and slowly, everything started to turn black.

# The Darrow Brook Fairies

\

**Oooam**

**She was over 300 years old, and was only 16" tall. She weighed less than a pound, but she was the most beautiful thing that I had ever seen.**

# Chapter 7

## Oooam

Still dizzy from blacking out after holding my breath for too long, I opened my eyes and started to focus.

Hovering about five feet in front of me, just barely off the ground, was a beautiful creature, the likes of which are found in fairy tales. She was about sixteen inches tall, scantily dressed in a pure-white lace, bikini-like outfit. She was unbelievably beautiful, with the cutest elf-like ears and long white hair down to her bottom. Her skin was perfect, neither skinny nor plump, and her smile was as beautiful as her face. I looked at her in amazement for a long time before I noticed that hanging around her neck, on a necklace, was Daisy's tag.

"Oh, you do have Daisy's tag!" I exclaimed.

"You are very pretty, Darbrie."

She curled up, smiled, and giggled as if she were shy.

"Well, you are," I repeated, "and you have a beautiful outfit on."

She coiled up again and quietly said, "Thank you."

"Darbrie is pretty?" she asked politely.

"Oh, yes, you are very pretty!" I exclaimed again.

With that, she suddenly flew straight up, then back down, then to the left and right, before stopping where she had started and slowly flying right up to me.

With her head back and her chest out, she presented me with the shiny tag hanging around her neck.

"You take," she said.

I reached out and held the tag between my finger and thumb. As I started to remove it, I let my hand move closer, so the back of my finger touched her chest.

Poof! She was gone.

I had just wanted to be sure she was real, and I may have blown my chance. But at least I now knew for sure that she was real.

A couple of minutes passed before she returned to her spot in front of me. I was terribly relieved she had returned.

"Jude Man touch Darbrie," she scolded.

"Oh, I am very sorry," I explained. "I just wanted to be sure you were real! I find it so hard to believe a girl so pretty could be out here in the swamp and be real."

"Jude Man touch Darbrie," she repeated.

"I swear I didn't mean any harm," I explained. "I will not do it again. Can you forgive me?"

She looked at me and smiled. She flew straight up again, then left and right, before returning. It was as if she were deciding, and she again flew slowly up to me, presenting the tag.

I carefully removed the tag, and she flew back to hover in her spot.

Smiling and extremely happy, I had Daisy's tag again. I put it in my pocket and zipped it closed.

I looked up and noticed she was studying me. I smiled and asked, "Is Darbrie your name?"

"Darbrie is Darbrie, Darbrie not name. What is Jude Man's name?"

"My name? My name is Bob."

"Bob is Jude Man," she let out a strange sound. "Oooam is Darbrie," she explained.

"Is Oooam your name?" I inquired.

"Oooam is not a name, silly; Oooam is a sound," she explained.

I smiled, not understanding at all. I unzipped my pocket and took out the tag, just to be sure this was all happening.

If this isn't happening and it's a dream or something else, I hope I don't wake up for a long time. I was happy, happier than I could ever remember being.

I polished the charm with some universal solvent, put the tag back in my pocket, and got a sandwich and a beer out of my vest.

My new friend was on the edge of the swamp, not far, looking at and touching a big red flower.

"Oooam!" I called out.

She turned and looked at me. I knew now that it was indeed her sound.

"Do you want some food?" I asked.

Oooam flitted over and looked at my sandwich. I pulled off a piece, set it on the ground in front of me, and continued eating the rest. Oooam reached out, broke off a portion, and retreated to her spot as before.

She ate the bread and returned for another piece grabbing and breaking off a piece like a bird would do.

"How about some beer?" I joked, but Oooam looked up and shook her head yes.

I didn't have anything to pour some beer into, so I looked around. There was a plant by the swamp with large leaves. I got up, and Oooam retreated. I picked a large leaf and, turning it upside down, placed it on the ground where Oooam had been hovering. I then poured beer into the indent of the upside-down leaf.

I returned to my tree and drank my beer while watching Oooam. She returned to her spot, landed, and dipped her face into the beer to drink. It was so cute to watch that I almost laughed, but I didn't want to spook her again. That was also the first time I had seen her land.

Oooam drank the beer, all of it. I might have poured her more, but she was already looking a bit tipsy. She flew up, then down, landing and flopping around on the ground, laughing and giggling the whole time. It was then that I realized we might not be alone.

"Are there more Darbries?" I asked Oooam.

"Darbries, Darbries, Darbries, Darbries," she answered.

"Does that mean yes, there are more?" I clarified.

"Yes, Darbries, Darbries, Darbries," she answered, laughing.

I heard fluttering behind me and looked around. I didn't see any other Darbries, but I knew they were there.

I hoped they were as nice as Oooam, I thought.

I spent the rest of the day answering her questions about me and asking her questions about Darbries. Her broken

English and unfamiliar slang made communication challenging.

Slowly, I began to understand what she was saying. Of course, Oooam was not her name; Darbries didn't have names. They were given a sound when they were born, a sound of the wind, a rock falling, or perhaps an animal nearby. It wasn't a name, but a sound to identify with, much like we give children names.

Oooam didn't own the tag she had found either. She liked it a lot, but it was not hers. It wasn't because it was mine; it was because it was a thing. She did not own things. A thing was just there or it wasn't. She taught me this by pointing out a small deer getting a drink. "Look!" she said.

She explained, in her way, that the thing was a deer getting a drink. I could not own that. The deer was either there or it wasn't. There was nothing to own. You couldn't demand to see a deer taking a drink. It wasn't yours, and anyone was equally entitled to see the deer when it appeared again. She explained that all things were that way.

It took a long time to explain that to me, and even longer for me to understand, but Oooam was very patient. She actually improved her English as we talked. It had been a long time since she had spoken English.

It was getting late, and since Oooam seemed sober now, I started packing up to leave, cleaning any mess we had made.

I wanted to stay forever, to live out here with Oooam and meet all the Darbries, but reality set in, and I had to return home, whether this was real or not.

I said goodbye to Oooam, and she flew off into the swamp with a blur. Then I heard the sound, the whoosh of a thousand bird-girls flying into the swamp.

There were more, all right, lots more.

# Chapter 8

## Jude Man Clue

I got up early the next morning. I wanted to go out and see Oooam. I lied to my girlfriend, telling her I was building a tree stand and had left a tool out there that I needed for work.

I jogged the whole way and was huffing and puffing when I reached my spot. Oooam showed up almost immediately. I was elated. I had been wavering between knowing the difference and telling if this was real life or just a dream. She would show up right away in a dream, I thought. I pinched myself hard, feeling the sharp sting, and it hurt. I wanted this to be real. I wanted Oooam to be real, but I still wasn't sure I wasn't losing my mind.

"Hello!" I quickly greeted Oooam.

"Hello," she sheepishly replied.

"I hoped you would come this morning, and you did," I explained.

"I heard you coming, Darbries all heard you coming," she giggled.

"I guess I did make a bit of noise. Tell me, Oooam, how can I know that you are real?"

"Real? Silly! We were here before you! We were here long before you," Oooam continued. "Is the fox real? Is the hawk real? We know all about the fox and the hawk. We want to know about you."

"Oh, I want to know all about you, too," I admitted. "I want to know everything about you and all the rest, too."

"Jude Man, big sign, four corners," she spoke, then flew off to the swamp.

I didn't know why she left, but I was somewhat glad, as I had to go, too. I hurriedly went home and readied for work.

"Jude Man, big sign, four corners," I couldn't get it out of my head. Although she didn't mean it to be a clue, that's all it was to me. I had no idea what it meant, and I thought about it all week.

Goodman, a guy named Jude or Judy, a billboard? Idea after idea flashed through my head. I remembered when I was playing Little League baseball, that John, Wayne, Ronnie, and Jackson always talked about "four corners."

I was driving by and stopped to see John. "Where is this four corners that you used to talk about?" I asked.

"Are you kidding?" John chuckled. "It's right here!"

"What do you mean right here?" I prodded.

"Right here! The four corners are at the crossing of Station Road and Williams Road. The crossing roads make it into four corners: northeast, northwest, southeast, and southwest, four corners," John explained.

"I can't believe I never knew that," I replied. "I always thought it was a name for a special place. I always called this crossing Duchess Corner."

"Yeah, it was Duchess Corner, too, because old Dutch used to run a store here out of the front of his house," John went on. "We all used to go there for the penny candy he always had on the counter. He always had lots of candy, and it was mostly a penny."

"I remember it well," I told him. "Mom would stop on the way to the supermarket and buy some of our groceries locally. She wanted to support old Dutch and hoped he would someday get gasoline for sale, too. We kids loved the candy, and mom would always get us a piece but would get upset with us for taking so long to choose. There were all kinds of beautiful, sparkling candies lined up in jars for us to choose from. That's a great memory, John, but I have to get back to work. It was nice talking to you again." And with that, I went outside and looked for the sign.

I couldn't remember ever seeing any signs around here, let alone a big sign. There weren't any billboards anywhere in Greenfield Township, as far as I could remember. Sure enough, there weren't any signs, and no reference to Jude Man.

I really didn't have to get back to work. I was late to have lunch with my neighbor Bill. I met him at the diner at Colt Station. He was waiting patiently inside in a booth.

I asked him about Jude Man or anyone named Judeman. He had never heard the name before. I asked the waitress, and she shouted to all the customers.

"Does anyone know of a Judeman?" she shouted.

I watched the faces of the other customers as they either shook their heads no or returned to their meal.

"Why, who are you looking for?" Bill asked.

"Ah, nothing," I replied, "just a hunch."

"Ask Randy," he said, "he knows everybody."

"Yeah, that's a good idea," I replied, and I changed the subject. I didn't want Bill to get interested in what I was doing directly behind the property he owned. He never went back that far, as far as I knew, at least.

I hadn't learned anything, and we parted. I went to my truck. On the way, I saw the craziest thing I'd ever seen out here in the country. There was a traffic jam at the four-way stop. Close to thirty cars or more were backed up or blocking each other, driving on three of the four sections of the road. Beeping and yelling, they all had numbers on the side of their car doors.

It was a rally, and they would proceed through the stop signs then turn around and try to go a different way. It was hilarious to watch, sitting angled toward the road, trying to get someone to let me in. It was a race, and no one let me in. I sat there as it started to clear. It was at that moment that I saw the sign. Right there on the right side of my truck was a historical sign.

## COLT'S STATION

**Judah Colt, Agent, began the
First Pennsylvania Population
Co. development here in 1797.
He set up the first organized
Settlement in Erie County. at
the head of flatboat naviga-
tion on French Creek.**

Pennsylvania Historical and Commission

Did I just find "Jude Man, at four corners on a big sign"? I thought I might have!

I looked up, and the traffic had thinned to just three cars trying to figure out which way to go. I thanked them to myself and figured that these guys, still confused, were not going to win the race. I, however, felt exactly as if I had just won a race.

# The Darrow Brook Fairies

# The Darrow Brook Fairies

# Chapter 9

## Two Week Vacation

Oooam consumed my thoughts. I could think of nothing else. I wondered if anyone could tell what was bothering me, but no one was paying attention. My girlfriend especially did not seem concerned at all. I thought that was a good thing, but I later found out why.

My brother-in-law had been working with me, he and his two boys. I also had two other guys working who pretty well knew the ropes. Jimmy barked at everyone all the time, mostly his boys, but he wasn't afraid to tell everyone to step it up or hustle. He was just like that. He could drive the truck and run the backhoe and tractors, so it was an easy move to put him in charge for my two-week-long vacation.

I told everyone who would listen that I was going to build a great tree stand way back in the woods for deer season. The location would be a secret, as I didn't want any disturbance around the stand to let the animals get accustomed to it.

The ruse worked, but I'm sure some people wondered why I was telling them all about it.

The next morning, Jim came and got the truck and trailer with the tractor on the back. I told him to keep it at his house and to work out of there if he could. He gathered up some hand tools and work-related gear and took off to prove his worth to me.

All he did was call me in the evenings and extol about how well and how much they had achieved that day. I really didn't care as much as he thought. I just wanted to go be with Oooam.

My girlfriend was coming home late and leaving early. She worked for a friend of mine at McDonald's, and had been promoted up the ladder until now, when she was the manager. This was a great job for her, the best she ever had, but it came with long hours and responsibility. Sometimes she had to both open and close the store. She was exhausted when she got home at night, wanting only to sleep. She got up early and went back to work.

She was far too immersed in her job to notice anything unusual about my actions, and I was far too obsessed with Oooam to notice that I was losing her.

# The Darrow Brook Fairies

# Chapter 10

## The Darbries

My girlfriend was off at work, and Jimmy had left with the truck, so I gathered some things to take back to the woods with me, including a full six-pack of beer. *I can put them in the water and keep them cool*, I thought. I reeled off some toilet paper and stuck it into a small box I was carrying. I then headed happily back to the swamp.

Once there, I put the beer in the water at the edge of the swamp. I set the box, full of treats that I hoped Oooam would like, and I waited. It didn't take long.

Oooam flew out and buzzed around the tree I was leaning against a few times before coming to a stop and hovering about five feet in front of me again. Of course, I didn't know it was Oooam until she came to a stop, but I expected it was her, and I was right.

"Darbries vote, Darbries voting!" she said.

"What's Darbries?" I asked.

"Silly Bob man," she laughed. "Darrow Brook, Darbries! Darrow Brook, Darbries!"

"Oh, I get it! You took the DAR from Darrow and the BR from Brook and are the Darbries! Way cool!" I replied.

"Darbries vote," she repeated. "Darbries vote Bob man."

"What do you mean?" I asked.

"Darbries come see, or Darbries not come see Bob man. Darbries vote," she continued. "Oooam come see or Oooam not come see, Darbries vote."

"Are they going to vote on whether you can come see me or not?" I said, frantic.

"Yes," was her only answer.

"You have to come see me! What will I do if you don't come see me? Promise me you will come see me anyway, okay?" I pleaded.

"Darbries will know," she explained.

"We'll meet far away, somewhere we can be alone. No one will know," I pleaded some more.

"Darbries will know. Wings will turn black," she explained. "All Darbries will know Oooam did bad."

"Oh no! Don't do that then." I worried. "Tell them to vote yes! Tell them they have to vote yes!"

"Bob man silly. Darbries know Bob man. Darbries all see Bob man. I came to meet you. Darbries all hide. Darbries all see good man, see Jude man, see Bob man."

"You'll have to explain that all to me, especially the Jude man. Is Jude man Judah Colt? Did your people know Judah Colt? From Colt Station?"

"Yes! Judah Colt! Judah good man. Judah help fairies. Judah help Darrow Brook fairies from others," she explained. "Jude man good man. Now Bob man good man. All the fairies will come."

"Fairies? You are a fairy?" I said quizzically.

"Seelie from Scotland," she tried to explain. "Seelie in Isle of Skye. Darbries now here."

"I thought fairies were very tiny, like a butterfly?" I asked.

"Silly," was all she said.

"Fairies know magic. Do you know magic?" I asked again.

"Bob man silly," was her only reply.

"And it's Bob, or Mr. Bob, please, not Bob man. Okay?" I corrected her.

"Okay, Mr. Bob. Darbries will come soon. I'll go check." And she flew off in a flash.

It was probably only five minutes or so, but it felt like an eternity. *This must be what it feels like to wait for a jury to come back with a guilty or not guilty verdict*, I thought.

I went over and retrieved a beer from the swamp. I popped it open and took a swig. It was too early to start drinking, but I was too nervous to care. I guzzled half the can.

I was just about to gulp the other half when she returned. She hovered out there and had a big smile. I smiled too, as I thought I knew what it meant. Suddenly, a Darbrie fluttered around, flew up and down, left and right, then stopped and hovered about twenty feet away, in front of me. Soon, another came, then another, and another. About twenty of the most beautiful creatures I could ever imagine surrounded me, waiting for me to do something.

I looked around, admiring their beauty, and said, "Hello!"

They all instantly flew back about a foot, as if they were connected to each other.

"You are all very pretty," I exclaimed.

They curled and smiled as they moved back closer. It seems Darbries all like to be given a compliment.

"Is this all of you?" I asked, thinking there were more.

"One hundred Darbries," Oooam replied. "These are my closest. They say yes. Meet the Jude man." She turned and explained to the rest, "It's Mr. Bob, not Jude man."

They all peered and watched my every move. Oooam landed and moved a little closer. Soon, one of the others landed, then another. I watched as about seven Darbries had landed and seemed calm.

Oooam started telling me the story of Jude man. All the others listened quietly.

"Judah Colt had a flatboat and one spring tried to go down Darrow Brook, to open it for traffic. I guess it was his job. We all knew them going down French Creek, but this was the first time he tried to go down Darrow Brook. Water was high, and..." she was interrupted as a Darbrie flew up and landed beside her.

"Others tried to come too," the new Darbrie explained. "Others were always trying to come into the swamp."

Oooam continued, "Yes, others tried to come. They were the Indians. But Indian boats were not flat like Judah's. Indians never got into Darrow Brook swamp."

"Judah made it farther than anyone had ever come down Darrow Brook and into the swamp. He made it almost to the Darbries' houses. Judah Colt got stuck in the mud. He could not get it out and could not go home. He was stuck, and the first night he was scared of every noise and everything that moved, even the ducks."

"Darbries watched as he stayed on a small high spot in the swamp with his boat stuck nearby. He tried but could not walk or get his boat out. He recoiled and hid when the duck's made noises in the reeds. He was scared of them until he explored bravely and saw that they were just ducks. The eggs were just opening, and he watched as he waited for fate. The next day a hawk swooped down, attacking the newborn ducklings. Judah charged the hawk that had landed next to the nest and grabbed the big hawk, throwing it into the swamp water. The hawk splashed around, then flew off, but it continued to circle."

"Jude man watched the hawk and the hawk watched Judah. It swooped down, but before it even came close, Judah was yelling and waving his arms while running toward the nest. It soon gave up."

"That wasn't all. The next morning, he was cold and the Darbries worried. He was huddled, trying to get warm, when a huge black snake slithered up onto his high spot. It was also seeking warmth. It was the very snake that had tried to get into many of the

Darbries' homes last night. The Darbries watched with content as Judah kicked it, then got around behind it and grabbed it by the head. It coiled tightly around his arm, but he reached into his pocket with his free hand and brandished a knife. He cut the head right off in one swift movement. The Darbries quietly rejoiced."

"It was then they had a vote and decided to help Judah Colt."

"Shhh was to approach Judah," when Oooam got cut off.

A fairy flew up, closer than the others, and leaned in. "I went up to him and told him I could help him get his boat free."

Shhh continued the story. "He kept asking if I was real and I kept telling him yes. He was amazed, but I told him that as long as he kept the Darrow Brook fairies a secret, we would fix his boat so that he could go home."

"He did everything I told him to do and promised that if we saved him from his fate, he would always help the fairies and never tell anyone about them."

Another fairy flew up and continued the story. "He tied long ropes onto the far side of the boat. That side was in more water than mud. He emptied it out and he started pulling on the rope without success. In a flash, all the Darbries appeared out of nowhere. They all grabbed the ropes and lifted up the side of the boat, flopping it upside down on the high ground. Judah turned it around, and the fairies and he again lifted and flipped the boat. They pulled until the boat was back in deeper water, where Judah packed it, said goodbye to all the Darbries, and promised to give us anything we need if we come to the station."

"And he did!" said yet another Darbrie that had come up closer. "He was always nice to the Darbries and kept us secret. You will too, right?" she asked.

"Of course," I quickly answered.

"Judah always protected the Darbries," Oooam continued. "He didn't hate Indians like people thought. He only yelled at them and stopped them from finding the Darbries. We would meet Judah at the Curve of French Creek, where Darrow Brook flows in. Judah taught Darbries about everything going on with the new people coming into the whole area. Jude man was a good man."

With that ending, I offered the Darbries some beer. I had finished mine and wanted another. They all smiled and said, "Yes, please."

I dug two cans out of the mud and found some large leaves. I poured the beer into the leaves, and the Darbries just watched. I sat back down and popped the top on my beer. As soon as I was seated, the Darbries all crowded around the leaves and drank the beer until it was all gone. It was so cute watching these tiny, beautiful, barely clothed girls drink beer off the leaves. More Darbries came in, and they scattered as I got up and retrieved two more beers. I got more leaves and poured both cans into them. Now they were all here for the beer. There had to be at least a hundred of them, well, exactly one hundred, if Oooam knew how to count properly.

The Darbries had a big party, laughing and flying around like they were dancing. They flopped onto the ground, laughed, and flew off again. They continued to ask me questions like, "Who you?" and "What you doing?" I tried to answer, but they usually flew off too quickly. It was an amazing sight to watch. It was like I was welcomed into a herd of deer, or maybe a pack of wolves, and I was watching them as they really were. That, except this was different. Way different.

Day one of my vacation had gone better than I could have hoped. I went home longing for morning to come quickly.

# The Darrow Brook Fairies

# Chapter 11

## Vacation Day Two

Morning came, and I was deciding what to pack. I was all out of beer, but I thought that was good, as I didn't want the Darbries drunk every time I went out to see them.

I did grab my hunting seat cushion. I had to sit anytime the Darbries were near, because when I would get up for any reason, they would scatter and disappear. The ground got hard around those old trees, and a cushion would help me be more comfortable.

I had lots of questions, and I double-timed it out to the swamp. In my hurry, I walked right into a trap.

I got to my spot, put down my cushion, and sat down, getting really comfortable before I noticed the whole woods were once again quiet.

"Crap!" I said. "Who's out there?"

I looked and I waited, but nothing. It was unnervingly quiet. I got up and walked around, scouring the forest floor and searching the trees. I saw nothing.

I walked deeper into the forest, away from the swamp. I was the only thing making any noise. I was about a hundred yards into the woods when I saw it. It was easy to see, perched high in a tree was a Great White Snowy Owl.

I instantly looked for ammo. I picked up some sticks and broke them, quickly approaching the owl. I yelled as I threw sticks at it. It didn't flinch. I threw more and harder, but the branches between me and the bird were deflecting them all. I couldn't get close, and it seemed to know it.

I retreated back to my spot and loaded my coat with rocks from my marker pile. I had a more important use for them, I decided.

I was about to take my rocks and go confront the owl again, when I changed my mind and went south along the swamp. I went further into the woods, and my hunch was correct. Not far from my spot, I spotted another Great White Snowy Owl. I ran at it, yelled at it, and pitched rocks at it. Soon it started to fly but landed again a few feet away. This was going to be harder than the others.

The first owl was much bigger, the leader, and was maybe the mother. I would have to scare her off first. I made my way back to the place I saw her and gathered up anything I could throw on the way. I thought about my .44-caliber black powder revolver that I had decided not to bring. *I'd get them with that for sure,* I thought, *but the Snowy Owls were protected.* I knew that. I would have been glad to see them if it wasn't for the Darbries. Ninety-nine Darbries was not an option.

I pitched some rocks at the great bird, but it didn't budge. I even hit it in the wing with a rock, but it just shifted its position a bit. I was throwing rocks, demanding its attention, when I heard the noise. It sounded like a big blast of wind, and the owl was being peppered with an invisible force. Feathers were flying, and when it tried to catch one of the invisible attackers, I threw rocks and got its full attention. It flopped down onto the ground, and I continued to approach, throwing rocks as hard and as fast as I could. Feathers still flying, it finally flew off.

"Follow me!" I said to my invisible army!

I ran ahead to the smaller Snowy Owl and pitched some rocks. It didn't take long, with the invisible attacks, and the owl flew off in confusion.

I was ready to rejoice and was calming down when both Oooam and Shhh appeared, hovering in front of me. They looked frantic and scared.

"There's another!" they said almost in unison.

"Show me where it is!" I demanded and off they flew with me running right behind.

I saw it at a distance. I yelled and waved my arms. I had few rocks left and needed to use them sparingly. Every rock I threw either hit the owl or got close enough to get its full attention. Between the rocks and the Darbries pulling out its feathers, the fight did not last long, and it flew off to find the others.

I was both mentally and physically exhausted. Fighting with the Darbries had become the most important thing that I would ever do.

I sat down and rested. I needed a beer. It was past noon, and I was ready to call it a day.

Some of the Darbries stopped with me, while most flew back to the safety of the swamp.

Oooam and Shhh were among the ones who stayed with me. They were all very nervous and scared. They looked and darted around, ready to flee. I told Oooam that I needed to go home and rest, and that they should go rest too. I told her that tomorrow, I would bring beer, and that if the owls were truly gone, then we would celebrate a great victory.

Oooam and Shhh agreed and flew off for the safety of their homes in the swamp. I was concerned at the expressions on all their faces. They were both angry and scared, and it showed.

I went home, cleaned up, and went to the bar. I had some beers but wished I was back at the swamp already. I couldn't tell anyone what had happened, and no one would believe me or understand anyway. I sat alone and drank.

# Chapter 12

## Vacation Day Three

I slept in. When I finally got up, I rubbed the drunk out of my eyes and took a shower. My girlfriend hadn't come home last night. I got both scared and jealous. I called her work. My friend, the owner, answered. He explained he was busy flipping burgers and that she had taken a few days off. She said she'd be back Monday.

"She does a great job here," he explained, "but I have to go now."

I called her sister. "Where is she?" I demanded.

"She went to visit the kids!" Tina shouted right back. "She left you a note!"

"I don't see any note," I explained.

"It's on your coffee cup!" she quipped.

Indeed, I hadn't had my coffee yet this morning, and taped to my cup, with coffee all ready to make, was a note.

*'Going to see the kids. Be back on Monday. Love you.'* And it was signed.

Shit, what an idiot, I thought. I was the one who came home drunk again. She missed the kids. They were going to be at their dads for most of the summer. It had been very quiet around here.

I gathered my supplies for the celebration, hoping the owls were gone, and wondered about the lack of a treehouse when the summer was over. I smiled to myself. I wouldn't be able to get anyone to walk back there and look at it, even if I built the 'Taj Mahal' out there. There would be excuse after excuse on why she couldn't come. It was a perfect ruse.

I grabbed two six-packs. I would have carried more if I could. I had a three-day-old cake that I picked up for two dollars at the general store. Someone ordered it and never picked it up. I told the cashier that I was going to give it to the birds.

"Good," she replied. "I put a lot of effort into making that cake. I hope someone, or something, enjoys it."

It was pretty mangled by the time I got to the swamp.

I made a pile and put the beer in the water to stay cool. The Darbries didn't show up right away. I listened, and the woods were bustling with movement and noise. There weren't any predators around.

I opened the cake box and inspected the damage. It wasn't as bad as I expected. It was smooshed a bit but retained its shape. I tasted some icing with my finger, and it was great. There were three candles on it, and it said "Happy Birthday" in bright red icing.

Some young kid missed out on their birthday cake, I mused. That's a sad thing, I thought. Wouldn't it be wonderful if he or she could come out here and share the cake with the fairies? That would fix the parent that was so neglectful. I made a mental note not to ever forget the birthday cake and closed the box.

I sat there alone for a few hours, enjoying the beauty and ambiance of the forest. It was then that Oooam and a few others finally came out to greet me.

"There you are," I said.

They were still worried and were darting and looking all around.

"It appears safe," she said with a tentative smile. "I hope they are gone for good."

"Me too!" I exclaimed. "Where are the others?"

"Some are still scared and home," she explained, "but most are scouting and patrolling. We have been watching all night."

"Everything seems okay?" I asked.

"So far," Oooam concluded.

It was around two o'clock in the afternoon before we could have a normal conversation. Up until then, they were ready to fly off at any second. It was nice to see them calming down and more joining the group.

I had many questions, and so did they. They wanted to know about everything going on, from new people to new construction, they were interested in everything. They spied a lot, all right, and they knew more than they let on, but they didn't understand the nuances and wanted all the details. What were the trucks and cars with the sirens for? The Darbries hated the sirens. I explained that emergency vehicles have the right of way, and they finally understood that it wouldn't ever have anything to do with them.

I asked them about Judah Colt.

"How many generations had it been since you met Judah, and do you know him from stories, or do you have books?" I asked the group.

They all turned to each other and whispered.

A Darbrie that answered to Woosh spoke up, "I know Judah."

Then another, and another. They all said, "I know Judah," or "I know Jude man."

"But how do you know him?" I pleaded.

Everyone just looked at me. Oooam broke the silence.

"All Darbries know and remember Judah Colt."

"But he died two hundred years ago," I cried.

Both Shhh and Woosh said, "Yes," in unison.

"Shhh, you would have to be over three hundred years old to know Judah Colt! Surely you are not three hundred years old!"

Oooam stepped in to clear things up.

"Neither of them is three hundred years old, Mr. Bob."

That was followed by a long pause.

"Shhh is three hundred eighty-one, and Woosh will soon be four hundred."

I was amazed. "You are kidding, right?" I said. "You are trying to fool Mr. Bob."

"Darbrie not lie," Oooam said casually. "Darbries were all over one hundred years old when we left Scotland."

"That's amazing," I answered. "How long do Darbries live?"

Oooam looked around, and they talked. Soon they came up with the answer.

"Darbries just live," she explained.

"But Darbries can die?" I questioned.

Oooam flew back. "Mr. Bob knows Darbries can die?" she asked, shaking.

"No, no, no, I don't know that. I was asking you!" I explained.

Oooam smiled sheepishly. "In Scotland, other Seelie Court fairies say maybe a fairy got caught and got eaten by a bear. Another tale says that two fairies got trapped and tortured by some humans. Some say they died. Nothing is true-true, it's always maybe true."

"Maybe Darbries can die, maybe not." And with that, Oooam suggested we start the celebration.

And so, we did!

I retrieved a six-pack from the swamp water and popped the top. All the Darbries were ready this time. They each picked a nice big leaf and lined up in front of me. They held out their leaves, and I poured them full of beer. Soon, everyone was laughing and telling the story of the Great Snowy Owls. Others flew in and joined the party, telling everyone it was all clear. Moods were all turned to happiness and joy.

I continued to pour the beer and opened the cake. The Darbries loved the cake. I threw the three candles off to the side, and some of the Darbries smooshed the icing onto each other in fun. It was a funny sight to see them throwing balls of icing and splattering it on each other while they ate the cake. They would clean themselves off in the water, then fly right back into the mix, flying and dodging the icing balls. They didn't get drunk like before.

Darbries love beer, but this was too soon after the attack to let down their guard completely. We had fun until sunset.

Some of the Darbries stayed after all the rest went back to their homes in the swamp. The ones that stayed, including

Oooam and Shhh, guided me back to my house in the dark. Holding the birthday candles for light, they lit my path through the woods. Others were flying above, scouting ahead. The candles lasted a long time. I learned that they had retrieved the discarded candles and dipped them in swamp mud. When the mud dried, the candle burned for much longer. The Darbries were smart.

I went to sleep amazed that the Darbries were that old and still looked like teenagers.

# The Darrow Brook Fairies

# Chapter 13

## Vacation Day Four

It was Thursday already. My vacation was slipping away quickly, and there was so much I wanted to learn. With the news that the Darbries were that old and lived that long, I realized how little I knew about them, and I suddenly knew that everything I had surmised about them could be wrong.

I took two beers with me and two sandwiches. Let the six-pack out there be for the Darbries.

I made it out to my cushion early. It was my new marker, but I noticed the Darbries had started a new pile of rocks for me. *Cool*, I thought. I also pondered my questions, why there were only girls and how they got here from Scotland. I needed to know if they knew magic and if they could shapeshift.

When Oooam and her many friends came out, I started at the beginning.

"Why are there just girls?" I asked.

Oooam didn't have an answer. They all got together and whispered. That is how it seems they answer a question when they don't have an easy answer.

"Maybe we were all just friends?" she said tentatively. "We all knew we had to go somewhere soon, and it was easier to decide to all go together."

"Did you go in groups of one hundred?" I asked.

"No, one hundred was just how many we were," she explained. "We didn't count until later, to be sure we were all safe."

"Did you all fly here?" I asked.

"No, silly. Darbries fly very fast, but not very far. Fairies need to rest. We could not fly to America. We did not know the way."

"Well, how did you get here?"

"We went on a ship, of course."

"You chartered a ship?"

"No, no, we hid in the big bags of seeds. Two to a bag. We all got into and waited in the bags of seeds. We went by two to keep each other company, and we ate some seeds for our food during the trip. Fairies can go a very long time without water. What little we brought with us lasted the whole journey."

"And then what?"

"Well, we were in the bags and rocking back and forth for a very long time. Some got sick, and others loved it. We were lucky, as we were almost always alone, and we could talk quietly to pass the time."

"It seemed like forever when the ship finally got to a dock and the rocking quieted way down. It took days to be unloaded. We could tell the workers were tired and angry, and we kept very quiet."

Oooam continued the story, while all the other Darbries were smiling and nodding. More had come out now, and the area was full. Most had landed.

"We waited in the bags for a long time too. The lucky break came when one of the workers was told to check the seed. Everyone burrowed in deep. He opened and checked a few random bags, and on the last one someone called out for him, so he hurriedly tied the bag back up. It wasn't tied tight, and come nightfall, when all was quiet, Poof and Dree managed to get out."

Two fairies suddenly flew up to me and landed beside her. "Are you Poof and Dree?" I asked.

They both smiled and shook their heads yes.

"You are both very lucky and brave," I told them. "You are both very pretty too!"

They curled and smiled and flittered around before landing and staying close by.

Oooam continued the story. "The two fairies hid in the shadows throughout the entire night. They watched and learned where the sentries went, studying their every move. They hid in the bushes all day, going without sleep."

"When nightfall came, the two fairies waited until the nearby sentry went into a tent to get some food. They burst into action. Poof quickly flew into the tent with the seed bags and started untying the strings. As the fairies emerged, they too started untying bags until all the other fairies were free."

"Silently they waited for the signal from Dree. When the sentry was away, she whistled, and five at a time, five on each whistle, fairies emerged from the tent and flew frantically into the night. They hid in the bushes and watched the others come out of the tent."

"Finally, when they were all out, when the count was one hundred, they stole into the countryside, looking for a new home."

Oooam looked around and said that there was more, but it was time for a break. I agreed and noticed that all the cute Darbries had found a leaf and were smiling right at me. I knew what it meant, and this time they didn't scatter when I dug some beer out of the swamp. They crowded around me, and I poured them some beer. Darbries love beer.

It was during this break that a Darbrie I had never met flew up and landed beside Oooam, Shhh, Poof, and Dree, about three feet away from me.

"You will want to think my name is Owww," she started. "We searched and searched for a new home."

All the Darbries were quiet and still. Owww was the unelected leader and had everyone's respect.

"We searched and scoured the land. Our scouts covered vast territory as we moved more and more inland. There were a lot of great places, and we stayed for a while at many of them, but they were all temporary and vulnerable for one reason or another. It had been two years of searching when we found Darrow Brook Swamp. It was perfect."

"The Indians tried and tried to penetrate the swamp but failed because their boats were not flat-bottomed. Judah Colt discouraged the Indians as often as he could. He said to the Darbries that his tale to them was he was stuck in the swamp for days and would have died if he hadn't turned into a bird and flown out to safety. That story caused the Indians to quit trying to enter the swamp."

"We took our name from Darrow Brook and became the Darbries. We separate ourselves from the Seelie Court and are now our own clan."

Dusk was quickly approaching, and Owww wanted to be sure everyone was safe for the night, so we said our goodbyes, and I headed off for home.

I ate a large dinner. My girlfriend had canned spaghetti sauce from vegetables and herbs from the garden. Everything in it was from stuff we grew, except the meat, and it was venison. The kids claimed they didn't like venison, but whenever she had to go back to store-bought hamburger, they all thought it tasted funny. They never ate as much when it was beef. I loved the sauce and always ate heartily.

With the finish of a full day and a full belly, I went to bed alone. The house was hauntingly empty, and sleep came slow.

# The Darrow Brook Fairies

# Chapter 14

## Vacation Day Five

It was Friday. All I could think about was the Darbries. I did have to call Jim and make sure all was going well on the job they were working. It was a big yard with quite a few new bushes and flowers, but they were already ordered and were scheduled for delivery. The homeowner would decide the positioning, so there wasn't much to go wrong.

He told me things were going great! Jim was in his zone when he was in charge.

There hadn't been a mutiny, so I figured things were okay. I forgot about work the minute I hung up the phone and rushed out to see the Darbries.

They seemed happy to see me too. Right off the bat, they started taking turns flying up to me and showing off their tiny lace clothing and underwear. It was clothing to them, but it looked like lingerie to me. The lace was exquisite, and the workmanship was astounding.

One by one they flew up, twirled around, and waited for my approval.

"Very beautiful," I would say. "Darbrie's outfit is very pretty. You are very pretty too!"

They would giggle and laugh shyly, flying off and landing and watching the others take their turn.

I had watched between twenty and thirty of the fairies show off their clothes when Owww flew in and landed nearby. They all calmed down, and she asked if the others were pestering me.

"No, I love them all. They really like hearing someone tell them that they are pretty, and it's easy for me to do, as each is as beautiful as the next. And you are one of the prettiest of them all."

Unexpectedly, for the Darbries at least, Owww curled and giggled.

Everyone was watching her when an even more unexpected event happened.

Oooam flew up close to me and landed on my knee.

All the Darbries, including Owww, Poof, Shhh, and Dree, gasped.

Everyone was still and silent, but the spectacle was not over.

Oooam fluttered a bit, then folded her wings.

All the others rushed up close to look. They were hovering in a semi-circle in front of me, at a distance of around two feet. They were stacked up four fairies high, all trying to see.

Oooam was now sitting on my knee and was smiling to everyone, but especially to Owww. After folding her own wings, Owww smiled her approval.

The first thing I noticed when she landed was how little she weighed. She was light as a feather, maybe lighter? Her folded wing had sent a signal to all the rest that she was completely trusting me. She was not ready to flee, but more than that, she felt secure enough to be defenseless and protected by me.

I fought the urge to stroke her long, beautiful white hair. I just wanted to hug her.

Owww watched closely, worried that Oooam's wings would turn black, but they never did.

It was a monumental occasion for me and the Darbries, because from that moment on, all the Darbries were far less scared or jumpy when I was near.

The rest of the day was spent with me asking and answering questions about them and me.

I learned that Darbries ate bugs. There seemed to be a lot more to it, but no one wanted to talk about it, so I made a mental note to find out more about the bugs at a later date.

I did learn that they didn't eat many at all. They didn't have a digestive system like humans. They didn't pee or poop. They seemed to have the parts, but not the function. Food was only consumed as needed; there was nothing left over. Water, it seems, was dissipated into the air.

I'm not sure of any of this. They aren't sure how their bodies work either. I'm just absolutely sure that it's not like ours.

They always follow me when I have to pee. They watch and like to see the stream of water come out. I try to shoo them off, but they are truly interested and not acting funny.

They do act out if I fart! They laugh and think it's one of the funniest things anyone could do.

"What that!" they would say, laughing and giggling.

"Excuse me," I always said.

Some of them would fly right up close to me, point at me and say, "Who you!"

Usually, they would fly away before I could answer.

If they did wait for an answer, I would say, "I'm Mr. Bob. I live by the hard road." Or I would say, "I'm Mr. Bob. I'm a friend of the Darbries."

This seemed to satisfy them, but they were always asking for more. They always wanted to know anything I knew about what was going on in the area.

Oooam explained it, "At night we always talk before we sleep. Whenever someone says, 'Mr. Bob said,' it gets really quiet and everyone listens."

I learned that they spent a lot of their time sewing. Making lace and clothes was their primary task. They all love to sew. They sew the tiniest pieces of toilet paper into their work. They sew the lace fast. The sewing is not very orderly or symmetric. They just seem to sew away oblivious to the design, but the finished piece is always perfectly balanced. Every piece they make is unique and extremely beautiful.

They like to bathe too. They are constantly cleaning themselves and primping. They put leaves and flowers in their hair and on their clothes to look pretty. They all want to be pretty, and they are. They wash each other. They look after each other. If one of them gets splashed with mud, Darbries will surround her and quickly clean off the mud spots. They are all friends.

It's not that they don't compete. Darbries are ferocious competitors. They love to win; they love to be the best. What they don't like is to see someone lose. They help someone sad from losing. They help them at their own expense. The thing

Darbries like better than winning is helping each other. This attitude gives them perfect sportsmanship. We could learn a lot from them on the subject of competition alone.

Darbries make things. Not just clothing. They make wonderful adornments out of the things they find. They like to put them in their hair. They make necklaces out of tiny gold chains they find in people's houses. I say 'find' instead of 'steal.' Darbries are incapable of stealing.

You call it stealing, and I may call it stealing, but the Darbries don't own things and can't comprehend the issue at all. They take things from each other all the time. No one cares or reciprocates.

The important thing to the Darbries is to make the things better. They almost always try to make things pretty. Darbries just wouldn't understand if you were angry with them for making things pretty.

Don't misunderstand me, they understand the problem very well. They are very smart. They know people will get upset, they just don't know why. Darbries snatch things at night.

# The Darrow Brook Fairies

# Chapter 15

## Weekend

There was a storm brewing. I could see it coming in the distance on Saturday morning. It was out there building up steam over the lake. Summer storms could be lethal when they bring down the cold air from Canada and stagnate over Lake Erie. It sits there for a while, in the cool air over the lake, collecting moisture. The storm builds up an enormous amount of water before traveling south. Burrowing between the very warm air and the ground, the stormfront transitions from the cool air above the lake to the hot air of the city. It picks up tremendous speed as it meets the hot air over Erie, Pennsylvania.

That would be a bad enough situation, but it quickly turns from bad to worse if you live out here where I live.

The storm, as it picks up momentum, suddenly comes in contact with the escarpment. The escarpment surrounds the lake, showing evidence that the lake was at one time much deeper and bigger. The blustering air is forced to rise as it travels up the escarpment. It continues southward and, as it does, it sheds most of its water content. That water falls onto my house. Not all of it, of course, but I get my fair share. With the wind and sometimes damaging hailstones, the storms can be quite severe.

This was one of those storms.

I couldn't see Lake Erie from my place, because of the curvature of the Earth and all, maybe if I was up higher, but I could see a long way, and this one was big. I had time to get supplies, so I headed off to French Creek General Store. I got bread, lunchmeat, mayo, and beer. I got three cases of beer. I also picked up a bottle of Tango. It was premixed vodka and orange juice, sort of like a screwdriver drink.

Okay, I was an idiot. It wasn't much for supplies.

I headed right home and waited. I drank beer and sat at the kitchen table looking out the window, watching the lightning as the summer storm slowly approached.

I wondered about the Darbries but concluded that they were here way before me. During the last couple hundred years, they had experienced many of these storms. The Darbries would be fine, and so would I.

The temperature dropped just after dusk. It must have dropped thirty degrees in one minute. It got cold, and the wind started to buffet the house.

I moved to the living room and watched TV as the storm pounded the house. I could see into the kitchen, but looking through the windows, I could just see darkness. I was watching the curtains slightly blowing, even though the windows were completely closed, when the electric went off.

The kitchen windows suddenly blew out, throwing glass all the way toward me where I was sitting.

I jumped up and watched. I was unable to do anything but watch. The curtains blew directly toward me as the wind and the rain entered the house. Rain was pelting my face twenty feet from the broken windows and I was shell-shocked. As quickly as it burst, the curtains suddenly got sucked out of the house, and the rain stopped coming in. It was loud, and it sucked the curtains straight out with as much ferocity as it had blown them in.

This dramatic portion of the storm lasted for about fifteen minutes, and it soon changed to a steady, heavy rain. The wind died down, and I dried off and went to bed to get warm.

I later learned it was a wind shear, and it caused a lot of damage. As I slept, the storm circled. It came back with a vengeance.

I woke up in the middle of the night, half drunk. I realized I was standing up in the middle of the bed. I looked up, and I could see the clouds passing over top of me. The roof had blown right off.

Maybe because the windows were missing or maybe for another reason, the roof section directly above my bed had been peeled open.

I studied the damage and went outside in the torrential rain to get a look. I came back in soaked. There was nothing I could do tonight. I was in the dark with no electric and no phone. I dried off and tried to sleep in the kids' room.

Morning couldn't come quick enough. I tossed and turned in the strange bed. Maybe it was the strange noises I could hear without any front windows or roof over my bedroom, or just the fact that the house was vulnerable and open, but I could not sleep. I did keep warm, and as soon as the sun peeked out, I got up and surveyed the damage. The electricity was out, but the phone had come back on.

I called Jim, and his place was unscathed, so he said he would load up and come help me board the place up.

The rain was drizzling but had almost quit when he pulled in with the truck and tools. His boys jumped out and ran around back to look at the torn-off roof. It was still partially attached, and with a come-along and a mighty heave from everyone, it flopped back down almost perfectly into position.

The purr of the generator reminded me I could make some coffee, and after placing flashing and tar, they added shingles and patched the roof.

"That was easier than I thought it was going to be!" Jim said as he drank some of my fresh coffee.

"Thanks for coming right over and bringing the boys. They helped a lot," I said. "I'll measure for the replacement glass, and you can drop it off at the General Store. Pick up some plywood so we can board it off until we're ready to replace the glass."

With those instructions, Jimmy loaded up the boys and took off. I didn't have time to go out and check on the Darbries, so I cleaned up the broken glass. It was scattered all over the kitchen and extended into the living room. I was close to done when they got back. It didn't take long to make the patch. A few saw cuts and some nails were all it took. It was darker in the kitchen, but it was secure and the house was warming up again.

I turned my attention to the bedroom. I washed and dried the sheets and a blanket. We had extra pillows, so I replaced them and hung the wet ones in the shed to dry. The bedroom carpet was wet, but there was little I could do about that, so I opened a window and hoped for the best.

My girlfriend was due back sometime tomorrow, so I was tidying up when the electric came back on. I went out in the dark and shut down the generator, stashing it in the shed.

What a crazy weekend. I slept like a rock.

# Chapter 16

## Vacation Week Two

She would be here with the kids soon; I had to get out to the woods quickly. If I was still here when she arrived, I'd have to watch the children while she went to work. Her oldest daughter was capable of watching them and my girlfriend could tell her to babysit, but I couldn't. If you have step kids, you know what I mean. That would be the case here, I just had to get out there and check on the Darbries.

Everything was fine after talking to Oooam. They were always ready for storms. They build their houses to be impervious to both storms and floods. They had just settled in and talked to each other. They could all hear each other in their homes. They have exceptional hearing and have a unique ability to tune unwanted sounds down. The Darbries were just fine.

Oooam was worried about me as she had seen the roof torn off and peeked in and saw the glass all over the floor. Only after figuring out that I was okay, did she head back for home.

We talked for a while and I felt my bottom getting damp from the wet cushion. I would have gotten up except Oooam had just landed on my knee again. I could not feel her weight at all. I asked her how and why she was so light and she didn't have an answer.

"I be like all Darbries, all fairies too," she explained.

Her English was improving by leaps and bounds. Oooam told me that they learned English when they first got to England, before the trip. They improved and got quite fluent during their first time in the New World, but it somehow changed. They started shortening everything. The shorter the better. The slang came in and before you knew it, they almost had a new language.

"After that whenever anyone spoke correct English, everyone would chide them for trying to be better than the others. They would act as if the offender was putting on airs, and would snicker and laugh. For the last hundred years, it wasn't polite, but that changed in an instant when you came to us," Oooam explained.

"Everyone wants to return to English, at least for now. Everyone wants to please you now. We all are happy to have Mr. Bob for a friend. They especially like it when you bring beer," she giggled.

I whispered to Oooam, "Can I touch your hair?"

Oooam looked at me quizzically then answered, "Why?"

"It looks so soft, and it's just so beautiful!" I explained.

She shyly agreed and turned her head showing the side of her head. I reached out slowly and carefully and touched her hair. Oooam pulled away then leaned in even closer. I touched her hair again and stroked it down the side. I did it again and then, losing control, I petted Oooam much like one would pet a cat.

She started to make a clicking sound; it was fast and methodical. It reminded me of a cat purring, except it was clicks.

Three Darbries bounded in, then more, suddenly most of the Darbries were surrounding us. Oooam had backed off my knee but they were all still curious about what had happened.

"I just stroked her hair is all," I told them. "Nothing to see here."

They still stared.

"Does anyone want me to touch their hair?" I asked the whole group.

They all backed up again almost in unison.

"Are you afraid? I won't hurt you," I explained further.

It was completely quiet and no one moved until one of them flew up to my face and pointing said, "Who you?" Then she flew off.

Then another one did the same thing, then another.

It got quiet again, and I stunned them all.

I quickly stretched out and pointed at one, and yelled, "Who You!" I quickly pointed at another, "Who You?" The Darbries were reeling backward, when I started to laugh and sat back down.

They all started laughing too, but I didn't expect what happened next. One of the Darbries pointed at another and shouted, "Who You!"

The Darbrie fluttered backward as if they were pushed and the whole clan laughed. Then another one did the same thing and everyone continued laughing and giggling. Soon most of the Darbries were pointing and yelling, "Who you!"

It was like a new game. It was a game with no winners or losers, perfect for the way Darbries play. They laughed and squealed and forgot about Oooam purring on my knee. It was a good time to say goodbye and head home for the day.

I got back to the house and found the kids playing in the backyard. The oldest daughter was watching them and was lying on a blanket on the top of the picnic table getting a tan and reading a book. They ran up to me saying they were hungry and so I went down to the pizza shop and brought back pizza for dinner. That satisfied them and they all took showers and readied for bed.

We put the toddler to bed and the rest of us watched some TV before I sent the boys off to bed. After an hour or so while she waited for mom to get home, I thanked her for her help with the boys and sent her too off to bed. She balked but I told her I'd let her mom wake her when she got home.

When I woke up the next morning, I was alone in bed. I went to the kitchen and the kids were all watching cartoons. The oldest was mad at me for not making her mom wake her up, but she got doubly mad after I told her that it wasn't on me, and that her mom never came home last night.

I called the store and she was too busy to talk to me. I called my friend the owner, and he said he didn't want to get involved. "You're my friend but she's my manager," he explained. "She's the best manager I have for any of my restaurants. I don't want to get involved or say anything that will upset either of you. I hope you understand." And that was the last time we ever spoke again.

I called her sister and Tina said that she already knew and that she was getting ready to come out to get the kids.

"It's all okay, right Bob?" she asked.

"Kids are fine, your niece has her nose out of joint. mom not coming home and all," I explained.

"Can you put her on?" Tina asked.

"Sure, here!" I ended.

I handed her the phone and soon she was smiling and even laughed a few times before saying goodbye and hanging up.

She helped me get the boys ready and gathered the stuff they would take. I gave her some money and told her not to tell anyone. I thanked her for helping and soon Tina had arrived and then they were gone.

I didn't want to be happy. But it was my vacation and I wanted to be out in the woods. I especially wanted to go out today as it was a beautiful day.

I dug my pack out of the closet and put some clothes in it. I packed a tarp and a sleeping bag. I filled it with cans of beer and added a carton of cigarettes. I had run out on other occasions and figured I'd leave some out there. I strapped a folding chair onto the pack, one that had a cushion attached. I'm tired of sitting on the wet ground, I thought to myself. I finished packing by putting a flashlight in one of the pockets and I affixed a lantern to the frame. The last thing I grabbed was my .44. I didn't strap the holster on; I just opened the pack and placed it in my waterproof box.

The walk out to the swamp was more difficult than normal, but I was in good spirits. It was a gorgeous day and I was thinking about the possibility that I stay out there all night. It would be scary, and I might not sleep at all through the night, but it would be an achievement and I'd have more time with the fairies.

I got camp set up, and I positioned my chair by the tree. The tarp was spread, with the sleeping bag on it and the waterproof box with my supplies.

The Darbries were fluttering about, flying in and out again, watching everything I was doing. I sat on my new comfy chair and watched as a few Darbries landed on my sleeping bag, then a few more. Soon the whole tarp was full and others seemed to want to get onto it too. I should have done this sooner.

One of the fairies complained. I had never heard them complain before. "No place for Darbrie," she said sadly.

Oooam flew up, hovered, and said, "Take my spot!"

She quickly settled into one of the best spots on the bag.

Oooam flittered over to me and once again landed on my knee.

"Well, hi Oooam," I said to her. "Don't you look especially pretty today." She curled and seemed to almost blush.

Owww was the last fairy to fly in. She looked around and hovered for a bit. She flittered one way then the other.

It was then with everyone watching, that Shhh said, "I know what to do!" and hovered and told Owww to take her spot.

Shhh then timidly flew up and landed on my other knee.

That was the first time I had ever seen all the Darbries landed at the same time. It was quite a sight. Ninety-eight fairies on my tarp and two on my lap. My smile almost split my face in two.

I looked at Shhh and said, "And Shhh is looking so very pretty today too!" Looking back quickly at Oooam and saying how pretty her bikini was and how beautiful her hair was. I didn't want to cause jealousy.

I looked out and exclaimed that all the Darbries looked extremely pretty today and they all squirmed with joy. I told them to come up to me individually during the day, and I would tell them whether I liked their outfit or not. They came up to me throughout the day and asked me about their clothes. I told each and every one of them that I absolutely loved their outfit, because I really did!

Owww started off the talking. "Darbries or Seely Curt do not know magic. We do illusion. We fly fast so fast you cannot see. We stop quickly and it appears we come out of thin air. We can leave so quickly that it looks like we can disappear. We bring things and drop them and it looks like these things come like magic, and when we snatch something so fast, it looks like the thing disappears."

"We might fly off quickly and disappear and then you see a squirrel, wow, we shapeshift! But not really. All Darbries magic is we are fast. We are very fast."

"Darbries are not Pixies! They are tiny. Darbries are much bigger."

"Darbries eat bugs. We do not have to eat many at all. Just a few every other day or so. Darbries are not supposed to only eat the heads. If Darbries just eat the heads then maybe their wings will turn black. Darbries are not allowed to collect the insect heads. If Darbries keep collecting heads, then their wings surely will turn black."

"I know that most of the Darbries have collected the insect heads, especially dragonfly and praying mantis, but they are not supposed to keep the heads. There is no punishment for collecting insect heads, but it is frowned upon. We want to respect all creatures, big and small."

"Darbries cannot love each other or other creatures. Their wings will turn black. Darbries are almost old enough to love. We are all starting to mature. We must be very careful around Mr. Bob, as he is to be looked up to but not loved. Oooam must be careful, Shhh must be careful, even I must not allow my feelings to overcome me. That is only for our men in our clan, and we have no men."

All the Darbries listened quietly. Owww was not their boss, but she was the most respected Darbrie of the clan. Her words were heeded.

Owww continued her speech. "Mr. Bob is only welcomed because he passed the tests. Just like Jude man, Mr. Bob was scared of even the little creatures in the swamp. He was not beside himself with phony courage. Even a mudpuppy could scare him off. When the true test of courage came, Mr. Bob passed with ease. He scared off the owl, then he chased away the hawk, both known enemies of the Darbries. He was fearless in his defense of all the creatures around the swamp. He said, 'not on my watch.' And that meant that everyone was safe while he was around and that he would protect them. He picked up his trash and made the place look nice, just like us Darbries. But Mr. Bob sealed his connection to the Darbries by joining in the war with the snowy owls. His later promise to keep the Darbries a secret is the final part in his conscript into the Darbries. He is our friend forever, just like Jude man."

# The Darrow Brook Fairies

# Chapter 17

## Vacation Day Nine

It was starting to get dark, especially under the giant hemlocks. I started to make a fire when Oooam asked what I was doing.

"I'm going to make a campfire," I told her.

"Please don't do that!" she scolded me. "No fires, please. Darbries will not like a fire nearby.

"Why not?" I asked. "Don't the Darbries like to get warm?"

165

She looked at me puzzled. "Why?" she asked.

"To stay warm," was the only answer I could give.

"Oooam not get cold. Not like you. I do not shiver in the cold, like humans. Darbries feel cold, but it is okay, just like warm sunshine is okay. Darbries get bigger in the sunshine, and skinny in the cold."

"I think I understand. You fairies expand and contract?" I wondered aloud.

"Yes, but we do not like fire. Fire brings attention, fire has smoke, fire can singe our wings!" she explained getting more excited as she spoke.

"Well then, I guess I won't be building a fire then," I concluded. "That's not a problem, it's a beautiful night and I have a warm sleeping bag. I won't need a fire at all."

"Thank you," she responded. "I must go now; the others are calling for me."

"I don't hear them?" I spoke.

"Of course not, silly," she said as she flew off.

"What, no goodbye? No good night?" I said to the darkness.

Oooam suddenly appeared out of nowhere.

"Goodbye and goodnight," she said and disappeared again.

Oooam was special, alright, I thought. I smiled as I crawled into my bag. It wasn't that late, but it was plenty dark. I lay there listening as the woods went to sleep. It was at this moment when I truly felt like I was home. Maybe home isn't the right word or way to put it. All I knew was that right there was the exact spot where I was supposed to be, as I closed my eyes.

I lay there for a long time listening to the sounds of the forest. I wasn't scared at all. The Darbries were nearby and would help me with any trouble I encountered. I thought sleeping near the swamp would scare me, but it didn't.

I must have fallen asleep because I woke up scared and grabbing at something crawling on my neck. I caught it and threw it as far as I could.

I was sitting up and breathing fast when Oooam appeared. She looked around and found the bug.

"Beetle-bug," she announced. "No harm, he is friendly." She hovered above me as I lay back down. "Goodbye and goodnight," she said again and *poof*, she was gone.

I lay there smiling and drifted off to sleep.

I got up at first light. I was a little stiff from sleeping on the ground and foggy before my coffee. I hadn't brought any coffee or even water. I noted to myself that in the future I would bring more than just beer. A thermos of coffee would be ideal right now.

I was pondering having a beer for my thirst when Oooam and Shhh appeared hauling a bottle of water attached to a string. They dropped it down in front of me.

"Darbrie find some water!" Shhh spoke. "Shhh likes it for my hair, but Mr. Bob can drink it."

"Thank you both," I replied.

They explained that they 'find' water, or they get water after dark from an artesian well across the hard road. They use it for their face and hair.

"I know where that well is!" I exclaimed. "It's across the road in the field. It's just a pipe driven into the ground but it's been flowing ever since I found it. It looked to me, by the amount of mineral deposits built up on it, to have been there a long time."

"Darbries always use the clean water," Shhh said.

Darbries use the water from the beer for hair too, Shhh explained somewhat shyly. "Darbries drink the beer and try to fly but flop on the ground instead." Shhh continued, "Darbries try to fly really fast and instead fly slowly. Too much beer is too heavy to fly. After a while the beer stays in and the water from the beer comes out. We spit it out into each other's hair to make it clean and shiny."

"Darbries love beer!" Oooam added.

"I would like to see that," I spoke.

"No! No, no, no, spew beer water is private, not for you to see," she said hurriedly.

"Okay, okay, private, I get it! I don't want anyone to see me spew beer either!"

"Ha, ha, ha, Mr. Bob knows," she ended.

Soon all the Darbries were out to visit again. Well, maybe not all. A few were always flying in and others flew out, for reasons only the Darbries knew.

I asked them again about the lack of boys here. The Darbries took turns explaining it all to me.

The Darbries left for the New World when we were very young. We were all around one hundred years old. We were a group learning together like you have with your school, except there is no school, just older fairies to ask questions and get help.

Boys have the group too. Boys tease us fairy girls and we shun the boys. That's just the way it is.

When the scare came to southern Scotland, most fairies decided to move. The men came in and dug around the whole valley. They were looking for gold, but a few stumbled onto fairy houses. Luckily, they ignored the findings, but it was only a matter of time. The fairies kept a step ahead of the miners and explorers but were running out of hiding spots.

Darbries do not know how it ended. We all agreed to go to the New World together, and we bid farewell. Now we are here.

All the Darbries will be near or over four hundred years of age soon. That is when we quit shunning boys and learn how to mate. It only happens once, and Darbries have many offspring. Twins, triplets, and even quadruplets are common. More is rare, but it can happen. Fairy clan triple in size then stays there for hundreds of years. We cannot mate as we have no boys and are not ready.

The talks lasted all morning and I ate a sandwich for lunch. I popped a beer and wandered around the woods for a bit. The chipmunks were getting used to me and I saw them at a distance all the time now. The birds were always flittering around close by and the crows usually left by mid-morning. Their crowing could get annoying and I was always glad when they flew off for the day.

I looked for a spot to build a real tree house. It would have to be close by, but far enough away from the swamp to not arouse suspicions. I surveyed the forest a bit more then returned to my spot.

There were some fairies waiting already. They were on my sleeping bag and on the tarp. They were playing with each other and laughing and waving their arms around as if play fighting. As soon as they saw me return, they stopped and acted all proper.

"Just like a bunch of school girls," I spoke.

They looked at each other puzzled as they didn't understand my reference.

"That's okay," I said. "What do you Darbries want to know about me?"

One of the fairies popped up and said, "How old is Mr. Bob?"

"How old do you think I am?" I asked her.

"Seven hundred?" she quickly answered.

"Eight hundred!" another shouted.

"Nine hundred!" shouted another voice.

"Okay, hold on now, I'm not a fairy!" I explained. "I am twenty-five years old."

The Darbries seemed amazed. They knew I wasn't old like them because they are smart. They just don't like to think about it, as I seem so much the same as them in a lot of ways.

It was my turn, so I asked about the black wings. I received a firestorm of answers. They finally started taking turns and telling me about when their wings turned black. They weren't supposed to talk about it, but they were allowed to talk about anything at all, as long as I asked.

"My wings turned black!" one of the fairies popped up and spoke. "I ate too many bugs. Everyone knew and did not approve, but I wanted to eat bugs so I did. I spewed most of them out, then ate some more. I knew I should not eat so many, but I just could not stop. Everyone looked at my wings, but no one got angry. I just decided not to do that again."

Another told her story. "My wings turned black too once a long time ago. I went up by the hard road, it was dirt then, and I saw some men having beer in their boat. I flew fast and tipped a beer that was on a large plate. The man picked it up as if nothing had happened. I then scared a big flock of ducks and geese and when they took off, the men looked up. I snuck in and drank some of the spilled beer."

"I know now that I could have gotten caught and the whole clan would have to come protect me, putting them all in danger, but in that moment, I just wanted some beer."

"No one was angry. Well, maybe Owww was a little bit perturbed. But I told them all I was sorry, and I think most were just jealous that I got some beer."

"So, do your wings turn back to white again after you are good for a time?" I asked.

"No!" came a choir of noes.

One of the fairies flew up to me. "Look at my wings!" she said. "My wings fell off just two days ago and they are almost fully grown already. My wings grow back quickly."

"Did they fall off or get pulled off?" I asked.

"They just fell off," she replied.

"Does it hurt?" I asked.

"No, silly! It happens all the time. We always shed our wings and grow new ones." With that she turned around to give me a better look at her growing wings.

Suddenly many of the fairies were hovering around me showing off their wings. They were all talking at once but loved it when I kept saying how beautiful they were. Darbries were cooing and curling and smiling.

I did not know that, I admitted. "Do you keep your old wings?"

"We cannot keep them as they go away so fast," was my answer.

"They disintegrate? How quickly? Are they firm enough to show me sometime before they're gone?"

"They last about a day," was my answer. "We can make a small part of the top of the wings last longer by quickly cutting off the top and dipping the cut ends into pine tar that we collected. After they dry, we can put them in our hair for decoration."

"I have noticed those decorations in your hair. It really makes the Darbries look pretty."

"They last like that for a couple weeks, but soon they too crumble," she concluded.

I had learned a lot about their wings, but the most surprising thing was yet to come.

"How do the fairies move them back and forth so quickly? Do they break off sometimes?" I asked.

Oooam had come out and landed on my knee. "We don't flap our wings at all, Mr. Bob. Our wings simply vibrate," she explained. "We can vibrate our wings slowly or fast. We can even vibrate them very fast for a short time. It's really very simple."

Not to be outdone by Oooam, Shhh landed on my other knee and continued where Oooam left off. "Our wings do not have to move very far for us to fly," she explained. "Our wings work like one-way valves. On the backstroke of the vibration, wings can move effortlessly through the air. On the return, they meet the full resistance of the air. It's a very small movement, but because of the speed of the vibration, it produces a great deal of power to fly."

Oooam asked quietly, "Don't the planes fly like that?"

"No," I answered. "The planes fly because of air pressure, not vibration. If they vibrated, the wings would probably fall off in mid-air!"

"Do your wings ever fall off while you are flying?" I asked.

"No!" Shhh replied. "We know when they are near to fall off, and we stay home and do not fly."

Oooam piped in, "We are very vulnerable right after our wings fall off. We cannot fly and are scared if alone or not at home. Our twins or our friends always stay with us the entire day until our wings grow back to be able to fly, at least a little."

"Just how often do your wings fall off?" I queried.

"Oh, it seems like all the time, but it is once in the spring, once in the summer and once in the fall. Then we usually keep our fall wings all winter," Oooam explained.

"Sometimes when a lot of Darbries have lost their wings all at the same time, almost all Darbries stay at home unless there is a problem. When we traveled here, we had to wait until everyone in the clan had gotten their new wings before we could continue our search for this new home."

"The loss of your wings is scary, but quickly turns to joy, as all of the other Darbries want to see and talk to you about the shape and beauty of your new wings. Big or small, we love to show off our new wings." After that speech, Oooam turned around and unfolded her wings so I could examine them.

"You have the most beautiful wings that I have ever seen," I complimented her.

Shhh repeated Oooam's action and turned her back. "Oh my, Shhh, you have much bigger and very beautiful wings too," I spoke, as I admired her wings. I would have to watch my words carefully as to not cause a jealous reaction from either of them.

It was getting dark already and I found my flashlight and headed for home.

# The Darrow Brook Fairies

# Chapter 18

## Vacation Day Ten

I returned home that evening to an empty house. No dog, no kids, and no girlfriend, but that was not all. There was no couch, no TV, no kitchen table, or chairs. The kids' bedrooms were empty and so was everything in the kitchen and the bathroom. There wasn't any food or beer or even soap. I was surprised that there were still light bulbs! My bed was intact along with my personal items and clothes.

My hunting equipment and camouflage was all still in place as was all my guns.

I spotted the coffee maker on the counter along with a cup and a note. 'Here is some coffee for morning, don't be mad!' is all it said.

I decided to not be mad. I'm not alone or lonely I thought. I'll go out and see the Darbries in the morning just as planned. I'll do fine alone I told myself. Exhausted, I drifted off to sleep.

It was Wednesday morning; I drank my coffee on the back porch. I sat there and admired the woods. I jumped into the pickup and went to the corner store and bought some staples. I got stuff for sandwiches mostly. I didn't need smokes or beer, I had plenty at the swamp, and realized that they too would be gone if I hadn't packed them all up and taken them out to the woods with me.

I threw the clothes that I had been wearing into the washer, and made a list of the things I would be needing. I switched the clothes to the dryer and headed for the swamp again.

I figured I had learned most everything I wanted to know about these fairies but all-day little tidbits kept popping up about their behavior and their actions. One of the things I learned is why they fly up then down, right then left before landing. It seems it's like turning on your turn signal before parking. They want others to know they aren't sure of where they want to land and like four-way flashers everyone knows to be careful.

I also learned that they have a system of almost continuous scouting. Fairies are flying around on a circular route keeping an eye and an ear open for anything strange or for any predators that could endanger the clan.

The Darbries are very peaceful and do not start fights or commotions with any of the nearby nature. Darbries do however fight ferociously as I witnessed with the snowy owls.

The Darbries attack with speed and numerous pokes, pulls, and bumps. They use their tremendous speed to avoid detection. They are unusually agile and almost always can avoid any strikes even the random ones a predator will start to throw into thin air. It was the 'almost' that intrigued me.

"So sometimes you get hit by the predator?" I asked.

"Sometimes yes." I smiled as it was Poof that came up to answer. Poof was shyer than the others and it was nice to see her so close for a change.

"Well doesn't Poof look pretty today." I said complimenting her.

Poof curled and smiled and continued. "It was just a scratch." And everyone fluttered a bit in recognition of Poof's injury during the fight with the owls.

"Oh, my! I didn't know you got injured, is it healed now?" I asked her caringly.

"Oh yes, it's healed up now just this scratch or you call it a scar. It too will go away in time." Poof explained. "I was scared at first but now I am fine again. My twin sister put pine tar on it and it started healing right away.

"Is Dree your sister?" I asked.

"No, silly, Dree is my friend, she helped my sister." She explained, "That's my sister right there," and she pointed out a fairy that looked identical to her.

"Ahh, your twin sister!" I exclaimed. "I'm very glad that you are all better and I commend you for being so brave in the war.

I wish to tell all the Darbries how proud of them I am for helping fight the Owls!

The fairies soon flittered off and few were left when I asked Oooam, while she was landed on my knee, if I could touch her.

"I don't know?" she answered. "I'll go ask." and she flew off in a flash. Once she flew off the others followed.

Oooam returned shortly and we were alone. "Well, can I?" I asked again.

No was the answer, but she had a strange smile on her face. "What are you thinking?" I said to her.

"You'll see!" she replied.

Suddenly Owww appeared out of nowhere and landed on my other knee.

"Mr. Bob touch Owww not Oooam." She explained, "Touch Owww's leg right here," and she pointed.

I reached out to touch her and she stepped back, "Gently" she ordered.

I slowly reached out again and gently touched her leg. It felt more like a balloon than it felt like flesh.

"You may push in a tiny bit if you need," she spoke, "gently!"

I carefully poked her leg and it pushed right in; there was little resistance.

"Oh wow, "I said, "It's like you are made of air."

"I mostly am," she answered. "You may squeeze my leg if you continue to be gentle."

I carefully squeezed her leg a few times and was amazed about how it felt. There wasn't any flesh, I couldn't feel anything hard like a bone. "That is amazing I told her, I would not have ever been able to guess that you were made so different than me.

We look so much alike and it appears that you are just smaller with wings, but you are a completely different kind of being. I never knew that about fairies!"

"We are like we are, that's all I know," she answered. "You be careful about touching any of the other Darbries especially Oooam or Shhh, they like you more and we don't want their wings to turn black over your learning about us. If you need more experiments, you be sure to call me. It will be best if it be me if anyone's wings turn black."

They flew off for the night and I grabbed the flashlight. I would need it to find my way home again. It was getting easier as I was learning my bearings more but it was still a task making it through the woods in the dark.

# The Darrow Brook Fairies

# The Darrow Brook Fairies

194

# Chapter 19

## Vacation Day Eleven

Thursday morning and I was on the back porch again, drinking my coffee. It was misty with rain in the air, and the wind was blowing cold, but I had to sit out here on the seat I had built into the porch. I had to sit here as there wasn't a chair or even a place to sit down in the house. Nowhere but on the bed of course.

I knew I should do something about getting furniture today, but I worried that if it poured down rain, things would get ruined.

My sister had offered me some stuff they had stored in the attic, and other friends seemed willing to pitch in some things. Steve even had an old TV I could have.

No hurry I thought, I'm still going to spend the day in the forest, I'll just want to sleep when I return. I'm not going to want to watch any television.

I made some sandwiches and found my slicker. I thought about the old saying about fishing. 'The worst day fishing is still better than the best day working!' It seemed to fit even better with visiting the fairies.

Everyone that came out was glad to see me. There were only a few and Oooam was one of them of course. They had somehow folded my sleeping bag and folded the tarp over it; to keep everything dry from the mist. Some leaves were positioned on the chair in an effort to keep it dry too.

I thanked them for their efforts.

"Are the others staying in their houses because of the pending rain?" I asked.

"Yes," Poof said.

Oooam was still tidying up and removing the leaves from my chair so that I can sit. "Here, a nice place for Mr. Bob to sit." she smiled as she spoke.

"What's the smile for?" I asked.

"Mr. Bob can't sit down at his house, so he can sit here with us instead." She replied.

So, you saw that, huh? I replied.

Darbries scouts all know what goes on around here. Usually, it does not affect us but when it does, we watch closely. Oooam explained.

We decided to go for a walk in the woods as the air was dreary and damp. We walked towards the back of the woods. It was just me, Oooam and Poof, and I really enjoyed walking through the forest with them. This day was particularly nice to enjoy the walk, as I could walk silently as they fluttered on both sides of me. The ground was just sufficiently wet to eliminate any rustling that would normally occur.

We had been walking for more than an hour, now moving up towards New York state, when a Fairie scout appeared and whispered to Oooam and took off again.

"Some people are in your house!" Oooam shouted. "Grrr, thought you might want to know."

Oh, gee, yes, thank you. No one is supposed to be in there. All the doors were locked." I said excitedly. "I have to go there right now!" I started running for home.

We were in the old part of the forest and it was clear of most debris and fallen branches. Downhill most of the way I made good time getting back. I ran down the path but the corn and the sunflowers I had planted were too high to see over so it was when I broke out of the path and into the yard that I saw my pickup truck pulling out of the driveway.

I thought my truck was being stolen until I saw the washer and dryer in the back of the truck.

"Damn! She took the Washer and dryer!" I explained to Oooam.

She didn't seem to care at all. "I wish your scouts would have stopped her." I cried.

Darbries not protect Mr. Bob's things, she explained.

Then why did you follow me if you weren't going to help? I asked.

"Darbries not protect Mr. Bob's things, Darbries protect Mr. Bob." She said emphatically.

"Thank you for that." I replied.

I went into the house to see the damage. It was heartbreaking. All the pictures were taken down and gone. All except one of Daisy. There were muddy footprints everywhere. My clothes that I had left in the dryer were strewn along the entire hallway and had been trampled with muddy shoes. They all needed to be washed again, but of course the washer and dryer were gone. I looked and they must not have been able to unscrew the hoses, so instead the hoses were both cut.

My blankets sheets and pillowcases were stripped from the bed and gone. Even the coffee pot and the cup and spoon were missing.

It was hard to keep from being angry, but I did. It was impossible to not be sad, and I cried.

The two fairies comforted me, even though they did not understand the tears. Soon more Darbries came and they too were somber.

"It's okay," I finally said aloud, "she can take everything, if she wants! Even the bed! She can take the chair that's built into the porch if she wants! Good luck with that!" I chuckled

The Darbries started to flutter and went outside. "We don't go into the houses during the day, she explained, "this was special."

"Thank you for the comforting words, I just hope she brings my truck back soon." I told Oooam, I can't even get new stuff until she does.

I went to call Jim when I noticed that even the phone was gone.

# The Darrow Brook Fairies

# Chapter 20

## Vacation End

Today was the last day of my vacation. I was stiff and sore as I didn't sleep well at all. I slept in my clothes with only a jacket to keep me warm.

I walked over to Bill's house. He always had a pot of coffee on and I explained to him what was going on. "She's got my truck!" I complained. "I can't go get a couch and a TV on my bike!"

"Do you have a tube stuck up your butt?" He asked seriously.

"No!" I quickly answered.

"Then you're having a good day." He explained.

Jim had the big truck, she had my pickup and the Camaro was broke down, but I did still have my Virago.

Bill and I talked for a while as I filled up on coffee then I took off for the general store.

I bought a blanket and sheet set for the bed. It had pillowcases and all. I also bought a blowup chair for a pool. It would do for now I figured. I grabbed a sixpack of beer. I wanted more but that was about all I could haul on the bike. I had beer in the woods still, but I wanted one now. I tied it all down to the sissy bar and went home.

Once home, I popped a beer and made the bed. It looked really nice and comfy. I opened the chair and started to blow it up. I blew on it for about twenty minutes and it was still not half full. I gave up and sat in the squishy blob and finished my beer.

I rode over to Bill's and told him I was going up to the diner for dinner. He told me to wait and that he would go too.

We jumped into his truck and I told him the whole messy story. I carefully avoided mentioning the fairies. We went into town and picked up the TV from Steve and the table and chairs from the thrift store. On the way home we stopped at the diner.

We ordered our meals and I looked over to my right and said to Bill. "See those two old guys over there?" Bill nodded, "Someday that will be us."

"I hope you're right," was his answer.

He helped me carry in the new furniture, and set it all up. He then went home and came back with a trimline phone that I could use.

As soon as I saw him go into his house, I called him.

"Just testing." I spoke.

"Go to bed!" he answered and hung up.

I had squandered my last day of vacation and I had no idea of when she would return my pickup. I called Jim and he would be here in the morning with the attic furniture. My sister would come to help and then take him back home. I reminded him to bring some coffee or a way to make some, and a cup too.

I sat on the back porch, until way after dark, drinking the rest of my sixpack. I had hoped that Oooam would come to visit, but that wasn't their way. They would come if it was necessary, but not just to visit. That would be way too dangerous as their guard would be let down.

They would come at times in the future, but not without a plan and a full contingent of scouts and lookouts.

I passed out and slept in my clothes on top of the new blanket. Who said the best laid plans of mice and man often go awry?

# Chapter 21

## The Last Weekend

Jim showed up bright and early with the boys. The boys hauled the stuff into the house while Jim and I drank coffee out of a thermos my sister prepared.

It wasn't too long as we were straightening up the place when my sis showed up. She had bought me a coffee maker and all the supplies. She also brought in a new dish set and a silverware set. She unpacked it all and set up the coffee maker.

"I thought you said she took all the food," she spoke as she stood in front of the pantry doors that were now wide open.

"She did!" I replied.

"Well, she missed the pantry!" Sis exclaimed.

I rushed over and peered into the dark shelving. It was indeed filled with food. All the canned vegetables from the garden were in there. There were canned tomatoes, pizza sauce, spaghetti sauce and much more. Potatoes, carrots, onions, and radishes, all the ripening fruits and veggies were neatly stored. There was store-bought food in there too. We called it our survival food. It was food we ate, but kept in a large supply, just in case.

"She still has my truck; she might be planning to come get this food too?" I surmised out loud.

"Did you guys have a big fight?" Sis asked.

"Nope!" I answered, "we haven't even spoke. She just quit coming home and sent her sister for the kids."

"It has something to do about that job." Sis explained. "I heard stuff, but I'm not going to say."

"What stuff?" I asked firmly.

"I don't want to spread rumors," she explained.

"Well, you already opened the can of worms, so spit it out. What did you hear?"

"Okay, but this is just a rumor, but I heard the young guys that work down there were getting extra special rewards from her for doing a good job."

"Are you saying what I think you're saying?" I asked.

"I don't know? I don't know anything for sure. I don't even want to say where I heard it. But they thought you already knew, and so I figure she thought you knew too."

"Sis, I've been too busy to notice anything. We haven't been close for a good while now, so I'm not even that upset over this whole business. I don't care what she did, or what she took. I just want my truck back. I told her sister but you tell anyone that talks to her that if it's not back soon, I'm going to report it stolen."

"Oh, wow! Okay, I'll tell her myself. We still talk, just not about this stuff going on. I figured she talk about it when she was ready, but I don't want the police involved." Sis finished explaining and the boys and Jim were already in the car waiting for her.

I waved goodbye and locked the house before heading for the woods.

When I got out to the swamp the Darbries were flittering all over the place. They were flying around and dancing and playing games. It was the end of summer party and they laughed and welcomed me to join in. "Dance with us!" some said as they flew around me. Others were flopping and fluttering on the ground when I noticed the leaves. They had somehow managed to get some beer cans out of the swamp and filled up some leaves. They were all having fun and I got some beers for myself and found the transistor radio in my pack. I turned on some music and turned up the volume.

Everything stopped.

I quickly turned it off, and Poof said that it was too dangerous to make that noise. She explained that while they like the human music, it is too dangerous to play without being on full alert.

Oooam and Owww landed and continued the explanation as the others all returned to playing and dancing. Soon the party was in full swing again.

"We can hear what we want," Owww explained. "We can hear far away sounds quite clearly, if we listen. We can block out a loud sound like that radio and still hear clearly far away. We can choose what noises we can hear clearly, and turn down the rest."

"It's much like focusing your eyes on a faraway target, and ignoring the other things up close and in your line of sight. You pick what you want to see clearly and the rest is blurred." Oooam chimed in.

"Oh, I get it!" I exclaimed, "but why stop the party for music then?" I wondered aloud.

"Silly." Oooam said as Owww chuckled and laughed. "It's because we all listen all the time to just the music. We can't seem to help it. The music always captivates us and we become defenseless."

Owww continued explaining, "If we sing or create music sounds with the reeds, we must have scouts on high alert and purposefully not listening. It's very hard and we have to take turns as we cannot ignore the music for long periods of time. We have to have a plan to go with the music."

"I had no idea." I explained. I'll be more careful in the future.

"It's not a problem, we just went on high alert for a bit, it's all back to normal, let's enjoy the party and games." Owww concluded.

Suddenly a Fairy flew up inches from my face, "Who you!" she shouted and flew off laughing. Soon another and then another, "Who you!" they echoed. We were playing the who you game so I quickly reached out and pointed at a solitary Darbrie and yelled, "WHO YOU!"

Startled so much she flopped on the ground as ten or more Darbries surrounded her pointing and laughing. The scared Darbrie popped back up and flew up and landed on my knee. The others became quiet as she shyly said, "I'm Paaah." Bravely, she got even closer and folded her wings. "You are Mr. Bob. Paaah loves Mr. Bob."

"I am so sorry for scaring you Paaah." I apologized.

"No, don't be sorry for playing with me. I'm glad Mr. Bob wants to play with me!"

"I do like to play with you!" I responded. "Let's play a different game! 'Watch out behind you!'" I shouted suddenly.

Paaah was not ready for that and she fluttered and flopped down onto the ground as she unfolded her wings and tried to take off quickly. Buzzing, flying, and looking around she realized that nothing was there. Paaah started to laugh and landed on my knee again, but did not fold her wings this time.

"Paaah is pretty?" she asked with a curtsy.

"Paaah is very pretty!" I answered sincerely.

She curled and sat down on my leg. She looked up at me admiringly and then just flew off joining the party.

I realized that I had a great effect on all the Darbries, not just the ones that I knew their names. Paaah was a new friend but I struggled to recognize her face as they were all twins or triplets and were all so beautiful, that I wondered if I could pick her out of a crowd.

I sure hoped I could. Her effect on me was profound.

I finished my beer as the party was winding down and explained to the stragglers and Oooam that tomorrow was the last day I could come out on a regular basis. After tomorrow, it may be a while before I can come out again.

I said goodbye and headed off.

# The Darrow Brook Fairies

# Chapter 22

## Emergency

I made a huge bowl of goulash. It was really good. It was the sauce of course and not the cook. I ate heartily realizing that I was glad the pantry was still full, but concerned that the pickup was still gone. I have the big truck but it was a pain to unhook the trailer and drive the monstrosity into town to go to the store. I called Tina again.

I'm sorry Bob, she wouldn't promise me anything. Her sister admitted, "She said she didn't care what Bob did."

Okay, thanks for your help, I know you don't have to help me, but you also know I'm not being mean or vindictive, I'll make the call as soon as we hang up. I explained at length.

"Okay," she ended and hung up.

I called the police non-emergency line. It was after hours but I got to speak to an officer.

After explaining the situation, I made some things clear. "She had permission to use my truck any time she wanted. I explained, I didn't know she was leaving and moving out. I don't consider that she stole the truck, even after she came back and took the washer dryer, I wanted to be amicable in the split. I hope you understand? I only want you to give her a reason to bring it back right away now, or I will have to report it stolen."

"Is it all in your name or is her name on it too?" The officer asked.

"It's completely in my name," I replied, "the title, the registration and even the insurance is in my name only. She has no rights to it and hasn't paid a cent for it; I even pay for the gas. It's my pickup truck!"

"Okay Mr. Richey, I'll go see her tomorrow, if it's all like you say, I'll convince her to bring it back to you. Where is the truck now?"

"That's it, I don't know, and I really don't want to know. Her sister knows and will tell you," I explained and gave him Tina's phone number.

I searched my hunting vest and found a beer. It was kind of warm but I drank it anyway. Sitting on the back porch I realized my vacation was nearly over. I had the best vacation a person could ever hope for. I learned unimaginable things and saw the most beautiful sights. Fairies don't always wear clothing and those sights and memories will last forever.

I must think of something to seal the deal, but nothing came to me. I finished my beer and went to bed pondering that very thought. What can I do for them.

I was sound asleep when I was awoken to the cold and voices. Some Darbries had pulled off my blanket and were holding it up in the air. Others were saying, "Mr. Bob come quick!" all at once, but not in unison.

Calm down I said to Shhh and Dreee, they were both talking at once. "It's Oooam!" Dreee screeched.

"Is she alright?" I asked as I jumped up and started to dress.

"She is alright," Shhh interrupted. "She broke her wing!"

"Won't she grow a new one tomorrow?" I asked in wonder.

"No," Dree explained. "She will have to stay home until next spring!"

"Next spring? That's a long time. What do you expect me to do?"

"Mr. Bob can fix her wing." Poof said out of nowhere.

"How can I fix her wing?" I pleaded.

Poof flew right up into my face then landed on the bed beside me. "Mr. Bob, fix the pump!" She then continued a list, "Mr. Bob fix the window, Mr. Bob fix the roof, Mr. Bob fix the truck! Now Oooam needs Mr. Bob to come try to fix her wing. Okay?"

I smiled at Poof, "Okay!"

I gathered up some things and told one of the Darbries to find my small shaving bag. After bringing back two gym bags she finally found it and I dumped it onto the bed. I put in some alcohol, and some paint thinner, not knowing what I needed to fix a fairy wing, I put in some superglue. I rummaged in the truck and found epoxy and liquid steel. I tossed into the bag any glue I had laying around including Elmer's glue and some children's paste, and started running.

"Not to run," Shhh said, "no big hurry."

"Come quick, come quick, now no big hurry, make up your mind!" I suddenly turned around and ran back to the truck. "Tell me," I asked, "is the wing completely broken off, or is it still broken but attached?"

"It's still on kind of, but it's hanging way down." Dreee answered. "It has a big crack! I looked right at it."

Great, I just might be able to fix it. I grabbed a ball of string and some duct tape and started jogging back towards the woods again.

Show me the way, I reminded them as I dodged the trees in the dark. They fluttered right in front of me and I followed their every move and soon we had made it back to my chair and tarp.

Soon four fairies carried Oooam to the high ground of the hemlocks and set her down. She walked over to me shyly worried that I was upset with her.

"Are you kidding?" I asked, "I'm just so glad you are okay! Now let me see what you did to your wing."

Oddly, she lay right down on her stomach in my lap. Her wing was broken alright, almost completely off. It had a long split and the ends were covered in pine tar. It took three Darbries to hold the flashlight.

I tried to wipe the sticky pine tar off in vain. Shhh started to explain, "I put the tar on there to stop the wing from rotting. Our wings rot quickly you know, but did you know we can cut the small piece off the top of the wings after they shed and put pine tar on the exposed ends and use them for weeks as decorations in our hair?"

"Yes, I have seen them in quite a few of your hair. So, you put it on here to keep it from dying. That was very smart of Shhh. Thank you, Shhh is both smart and pretty." And Shhh giggled.

I struggled to get the tar off her wing, it still had a layer of tar no matter how much I wiped, so I reached into my bag and removed the paint thinner. "This might sting," I told Oooam, but Fairies don't have pain like that so she didn't even flinch as the solvent quickly dissolved the tar, but left the wing sparkling. I applied some alcohol to remove the paint thinner and after it dried, applied a liberal amount of superglue to the break. I had the Darbries hold the wing in its proper place and I wrapped the split break tightly with string. Around and around I neatly added row after row, to hold the break in place. I finished by putting a thin layer of epoxy on and it soaked into the string clamp, holding everything in place.

They manually folded her wings and I sat there with her lying on my lap until morning. I stroked her hair and petted her while she clicked.

Everyone could hear Oooam clicking during the night and most probably thought that her wings, if the patch worked, would surely turn black.

In late morning, they carried Oooam back to her house and I said goodbye. I wanted her to keep her wings folded and still for a day while the epoxy dried. I told her to try slowly at first and to be careful until she was sure that the patch would hold. I also told her that if it failed and broke again, that I had more ideas that were sure to work. And that brightened up her mood.

I walked home exhausted and decided to nap. As I was laying down, I realized that I had just done the thing I was hoping to do today, by fixing Oooam's wing, I had sealed the deal.

# The Darrow Brook Fairies

# Chapter 23

## The End of the Story

Well, that's how I met the Darrow Brook Fairies. It wasn't the last time I ever saw them of course but it was never quite the same as the two-week vacation. During that vacation, I learned amazing thing after amazing thing. My head was constantly filled with unbelievable happenings.

I visited them often, usually bringing them beer, but the dream was never the same. My heart didn't flutter anymore and

235

I lost all desire to tell anyone anything about my friends in the woods.

Whether they would believe me or not, I no longer cared. Just like Jonah Colt took the secret of the Darrow Brook Fairies to his grave, I too fully intended to keep their secret forever.

Before I forget, Oooam's wings worked perfectly fine and she kept the tips dipped in pine tar long after they fell off the next spring. They were white as snow the entire time. All the Darbries were amazed and realized that they learned something about right and wrong.

They knew in their hearts, if Darbries have a heart, that she didn't do anything that was bad or wrong, but were sure her wings would turn black because of old saying and rules. When they didn't, Oooam's stature in the clan went way up instead of down. That is one of the only things I take any credit on, all the other things we learned together are because of them. Darbries are incredible creatures.

So, to continue where I left off, I would not be writing this book if the Darbries didn't approve. I wouldn't tell this story without their one hundred percent consent. They voted of course and it was unanimous. Everyone agreed that I should tell the story.

You see, the Darbries will always be Darbries, even though they no longer live in the Darrow Brook swamp.

They weren't afraid of the swamp drying up or the creeks being dammed up, as I kept them well informed about the laws and the reasons that the swamps could not be drained. They were wary of all the people that now lived around the neighborhood but did not get scared enough to leave until the witch moved in. The closest house to the swamp was occupied by a witch. They knew she was a witch as she played with dead things with joy. She surrounded herself with dead things and was always cooking a pot of dead things and making who knows what, in a huge pot. The air around the whole house was pungent with the stench of dead animals, and the Darbries hated being anywhere near that stench.

They heard her singing scary songs and praying scary prayers. She chanted and grunted as she hauled more dead things into her room.

Afraid of the spells she might put on the Darbries if she learned of their presence, and afraid of the potions that could spill into the water of the swamp, the Darbries decided to move.

I had long since sold my property, unwillingly of course, and moved far away. I could not be called upon to help them so the scouts took off, to either find a new home or a place to stay while they continued to look for a new, bigger and better place to live.

Because of the witch, they packed and left. It was easy for the fairies to pack; they didn't have much to pack. They took their needles for sewing, toothpicks for defense, and extra clothing, the clothing that they could not fit, over their clothes, that they already put on, over their clothes. They hung things around their necks as they flew. I didn't see this but I know how they would carry things.

I know about all there is to know about Darbries. I don't mean to brag, but I learned everything I could about them. Me and Jonah, and he's been dead for hundreds of years. It makes me the world's expert on the Darrow Brook Fairies.

I don't know anything about fairies. Good ones, bad ones, big ones or little ones, there is not much I have to say, except if you believe in them or have seen them then good for you, I believe your every word. I have to, if I expect you to believe my word. I don't know about leprechauns or spirits either or any other creature real or imagined. I have never had any desire to learn about these things. I still don't have any great desire, except if you know about the Seely court fairies. If you know about the Fairies that the Darbries split off from, now that would be exciting to me. I'd love to get this book to them so they can know how the Darbries are doing! But that is just speculation, I've never heard of anyone that knows about fairies from firsthand experience other than someone trying to make a buck on the information. I assure you; I seek neither fame nor fortune.

The reason I write this book will become very clear soon.

What follows in this book is some reasons I've compiled for believing in fairies, and also, I've included some beautiful pictures of my fairy friends. These are not actual pictures of them but Artificially Generated photos, of what I remember they looked like. The names that I attach just indicate what the individual Darbries looked like so many years ago. The main thing I hope that you take with you after finishing reading this book, is that you know that I do not care one bit if you believe this book is true or not! I just want you to take the lesson with you, in your life, that someday, if you're both scared and brave, like I was, if you are kind and can be trusted, like I was, if you will fight for your new friends, then someone may secretly see that, and help you in ways you will never be able to understand or pay back.

Take that knowledge and experience

with you to the grave, unless otherwise instructed.

Soon. I will share my "otherwise instructions" with you.

# Believe it or Not

## Could Fairies be Real

Think about this with an open mind, I'm not trying to convince you of anything. I will just say the facts and you can add them up any way you want. I do want to thank you for taking this time to learn.

I have worked out a little chart that compares what we know about fairies to what we know about Bigfoot. This exemplifies the facts as the two species are so very different.

Add your own notes to the list. Challenge the data, do your own research. You might just find that you change your mind, one way or the other. It doesn't matter which way that you believe, it only matters that you make a learned and logical decision based on truth.

# Fairies' vs Bigfoot

## Fairies

1) Fairies are small. between 12" and 16" tall.

2) Fairies are quiet. They fly almost silently.

3) Fairies don't leave signs or tracks.

4) Fairies have exceptionally good hearing.

5) Fairies speak many languages.

6) Fairies communicate with each other silently.

7) Fairies are very intelligent.

8) Fairies are clever, they are hard to detect.

9) Fairies are industrious and make their own lace clothing.

10) Fairies create invisible entrances to their houses.

11) Fairies live in the most impassable swamp.

12) Fairies are very clean and without any odor.

13) Fairies live in large clans protecting each other.

These are just some of the many Fairy characteristics.

b

# Fairies' vs Bigfoot

## Bigfoot

1) Bigfoot is huge, estimated at 7' tall

2) Bigfoot is noisy, people hear him at great distances.

3) Bigfoot leaves huge tracks.

4) Bigfoot doesn't exhibit and great senses especially not hearing.

5) Bigfoot grunts and howls.

6) Bigfoot doesn't appear to communicate with anything.

7) Bigfoot is smart and wary, but not exceptionally intelligent.

8) Bigfoot may be somewhat clever, but not overly so.

9) Bigfoot is not industrious and doesn't appear to make anything.

10) Bigfoot is nomadic. He does not create a home or den

11) Bigfoot lives in large forests with old tree growth.

12) Bigfoot give off a distinct foul odor.

13) Bigfoot is solitary.

Some of Bigfoot's characteristics.

In conclusion, obviously, Bigfoot would be much easier to find. Any investigation or expedition would be most advantageous to look for Bigfoot. On a dollar to success ratio, the odds are far tuned to Bigfoot's favor.

Finding fairies, or Darbries in particular, is a much different situation. To travel to and search the most remote and inaccessible places only to find a swamp that is too liquid to traverse and too muddy for boats will present a significant barrier. Combined with the dense, intertwined plant growth, even penetration is fruitless, as you could be inches from the target and never see it. Even stepping upon a fairy house would not be successful. They can hide easily for months, while you have hours to escape.

In the unlikely event of a war with the Darbries, you will not see what stings you. Like an immense bee attack, you will be poked with toothpicks so quickly, furiously, and relentlessly that defense is near impossible. The Darbries will not kill you! The hawks and buzzards will. The many dangerous creatures like snakes, eels, leeches, and flies will devour you and pollute your blood. If you are ever lying in the swamp dying, remember this: I gave them the toothpicks! But even if you manage to escape, you will undoubtedly succumb to the fever and disease.

Go look for Bigfoot.

f

# Epilogue

This memoir is as close to the truth as I can remember. It's been fifty years since this story unfolded in front of my eyes, and I've kept it a secret until now. I would have taken it to the grave except for the Darbries' consent to tell the tale. They want me to speak up! They want people to know their true nature and ways. They hope for a day when they can expose themselves without fear, to the entire population.

They are not afraid of being found or detected. They are confident in their hidden world and equally confident in their ability to hide or fight off attackers.

Now that they've moved from Darrow Brook to an even more secure place, they want to dispel some of the myths that, at times, even they spread, and the rumors that portray them to be dangerous. They want me to convey how peaceful, pleasant, carefree, delightful, and loving they can be. I hope I've done that.

The Darbries are the most wonderful thing that has come into my life, and I am happy to say the relationship is not over. I cannot speak of the coming adventures, only to say you will be astounded.

Watch closely for information on the coming events, and I will dispatch the news as soon as it's safe to do so.

Until then, be safe, scared, brave, and sincere. Be tight-lipped and take your promises to the grave.

# The Darrow Brook Fairies

# The Darrow Brook Fairies

j

k

# TWISTED TRUTH
# PRESS